Mrs. Jeffries on the Ball
A festive jubilee turns into a fatal affair—and Mrs. Jeffries must find the guilty party . . .

Mrs. Jeffries on the Trail
Why was Annie Shields out selling flowers so late on a foggy night? And more importantly, who killed her while she was doing it? It's up to Mrs. Jeffries to sniff out the clues . . .

Mrs. Jeffries Plays the Cook
Mrs. Jeffries finds herself doing double duty: cooking for the inspector's household and trying to cook a killer's goose . . .

Mrs. Jeffries and the Missing Alibi
When Inspector Witherspoon becomes the main suspect in a murder, Scotland Yard refuses to let him investigate. But no one said anything about Mrs. Jeffries . . .

Mrs. Jeffries Stands Corrected
When a local publican is murdered, and Inspector Witherspoon botches the investigation, trouble starts to brew for Mrs. Jeffries . . .

Mrs. Jeffries Takes the Stage
After a theatre critic is murdered, Mrs. Jeffries uncovers the victim's secret past: a real-life drama more compelling than any stage play . . .

Mrs. Jeffries Questions the Answers
Hannah Cameron was not well-liked. But were her friends or family the sort to stab her in the back? Mrs. Jeffries must really tiptoe around this time—or it could be a matter of life and death . . .

Mrs. Jeffries Reveals Her Art
Mrs. Jeffries has to work double-time to find a missing model *and* a killer. And she'll have to get her whole staff involved—before someone else becomes the next subject . . .

Mrs. Jeffries Takes the Cake
The evidence was all there: a dead body, two dessert plates, and a gun. As if Mr. Ashbury had been sharing cake with his own killer. Now Mrs. Jeffries will have to do some snooping around—to dish up clues . . .

Mrs. Jeffries Rocks the Boat
Mirabelle had traveled by boat all the way from Australia to visit her sister—only to wind up murdered. Now Mrs. Jeffries must solve the case—and it's sink or swim . . .

Mrs. Jeffries Weeds the Plot
Three attempts have been made on Annabeth Gentry's life. Is it due to her recent inheritance, or was it because her bloodhound dug up the body of a murdered thief? Mrs. Jeffries will have to sniff out some clues before the plot thickens . . .

MORE MYSTERIES FROM THE
BERKLEY PUBLISHING GROUP . . .

SISTER FREVISSE MYSTERIES: Medieval mystery in the tradition of Ellis Peters . . .

by Margaret Frazer

THE NOVICE'S TALE

THE SERVANT'S TALE

THE OUTLAW'S TALE

THE BISHOP'S TALE

THE BOY'S TALE

THE MURDERER'S TALE

THE PRIORESS' TALE

THE MAIDEN'S TALE

THE REEVE'S TALE

THE SQUIRE'S TALE

PENNYFOOT HOTEL MYSTERIES: In Edwardian England, death takes a seaside holiday . . .

by Kate Kingsbury

ROOM WITH A CLUE

SERVICE FOR TWO

CHECK-OUT TIME

DEATH WITH RESERVATIONS

DO NOT DISTURB

EAT, DRINK, AND BE BURIED

GROUNDS FOR MURDER

DYING ROOM ONLY

PAY THE PIPER

CHIVALRY IS DEAD

RING FOR TOMB SERVICE

MAID TO MURDER

GLYNIS TRYON MYSTERIES: The highly acclaimed series set in the early days of the women's rights movement . . . "Historically accurate and telling."—Sara Paretsky

by Miriam Grace Monfredo

SENECA FALLS INHERITANCE

BLACKWATER SPIRITS

NORTH STAR CONSPIRACY

THROUGH A GOLD EAGLE

THE STALKING-HORSE

MUST THE MAIDEN DIE

SISTERS OF CAIN

MARK TWAIN MYSTERIES: "Adventurous . . . Replete with genuine tall tales from the great man himself."—*Mostly Murder*

by Peter J. Heck

DEATH ON THE MISSISSIPPI

A CONNECTICUT YANKEE IN

   CRIMINAL COURT

THE PRINCE AND THE PROSECUTOR

GUILTY ABROAD

THE MYSTERIOUS STRANGLER

MAGGIE MAGUIRE MYSTERIES: A thrilling new series . . .

by Kate Bryan

MURDER AT BENT ELBOW

A RECORD OF DEATH

MURDER ON THE BARBARY COAST

MRS. JEFFRIES
PINCHES THE POST

EMILY BRIGHTWELL

BERKLEY PRIME CRIME, NEW YORK

This is a work of fiction. Names, characters, places, and incidents are either the product of the author's imagination or are used fictitiously, and any resemblance to actual persons, living or dead, business establishments, events, or locales is entirely coincidental.

MRS. JEFFRIES PINCHES THE POST

A Berkley Prime Crime Book / published by arrangement with the author

PRINTING HISTORY
Berkley Prime Crime edition / June 2001

The Penguin Putnam Inc. World Wide Web site address is www.penguinputnam.com

ISBN: 0-425-18004-2

Berkley Prime Crime Books are published by The Berkley Publishing Group, a division of Penguin Putnam Inc., 375 Hudson Street, New York, New York 10014.
The name BERKLEY PRIME CRIME and the BERKLEY PRIME CRIME design are trademarks belonging to Penguin Putnam Inc.

PRINTED IN THE UNITED STATES OF AMERICA

10 9 8 7 6 5 4 3 2 1

For Sandra Elaine Diamond—
the "Princess of Quite-a-Lot" and
one of the nicest, kindest people in the world.

Thanks for all the good conversations
and great laughs.

The Emily Brightwell Web site address is
www.emilybrightwell.com

CHAPTER 1

"I'm afraid there isn't much hope," Dr. Douglas Wiltshire said, as he and his companion walked down the long hall. He glanced at the closed sickroom door. Oscar Daggett, the world's worst hypochondriac, was currently lying in his sickbed suffering from a mild case of indigestion.

"Have you tried everything, sir?" Mrs. Benchley, the housekeeper for Oscar Daggett, asked.

"Everything. There's nothing left to be done. Sad as it is, all living things only have so much time allotted to them on this earth. When it's over, death is inevitable."

"It seems such a shame, sir. You've worked so hard to keep the old stick alive, too."

"Even I'm not a miracle worker, and my best efforts simply weren't good enough this time, Mrs. Benchley. It's nature's way, I suppose." He shrugged and smiled as a young maid carrying a stack of linens slipped into the sick man's room. Dr. Wiltshire knew he ought to check on his patient before he left, but he really didn't see the point. He'd already told Daggett he was going to be fine. Besides, he simply wasn't up to listening to the man whine.

Except for the indigestion, there wasn't a thing wrong with the fellow. But Daggett would moan and wail as if he had the grim reaper nipping at his heels.

Dr. Wiltshire and Oscar Daggett had played this game many times. Daggett ate too much, drank too much, smoked too much and took absolutely no exercise. Was it any wonder he felt ill most of the time?

"I will see you out, Doctor," Mrs. Benchley said. They'd reached the landing. The housekeeper wasn't surprised the good doctor hadn't poppped in to say good-bye to her employer. If Mr. Daggett caught sight of the man again, he'd bend his ear for hours about his various aches and pains.

"That won't be necessary, Mrs. Benchley." The doctor cast one last glance over his shoulder. "I'm sure you're very busy. But do remind Mr. Daggett of my orders. He's not to have anything to eat today except clear broth and light toast." He smiled to himself as he gave the housekeeper instructions. As Daggett's complaints were actually very mild, there was no reason he couldn't eat a plain, but decent dinner. But Wiltshire wanted the man to suffer a little for dragging him away from his surgery and the genuinely ill patients he'd had to put off.

"Yes, Doctor. And again, I'm terribly sorry your orange tree is dying. I know it was the pride of your conservatory. I do hope Mrs. Wiltshire isn't taking it too hard."

Inside the sickroom, the maid stepped up to the bed. "Here's some fresh linens, sir, and a clean nightshirt. If you'd like me to help you to the chair, sir, I'll change the bed." She'd already changed the linens once today and this was his third fresh nightshirt. She hoped the doctor had given the silly old fool something to make him sleep. She wasn't sure how many more times she could change this ruddy bed. Her back was killing her.

Oscar Daggett, a corpulent fellow with a mottled complexion and thinning blond hair, lifted his head from the six overstuffed pillows. His watery gray eyes were as big as saucers and his expression panic-stricken. "My box, Nelda. Bring me my box. Hurry."

"What box, sir?" She laid the linens on the bedside table.

He threw out his arm, pushing the heavy, red-velvet bedcurtains to one side and pointed at the huge armoire opposite the windows. "My letter box. I must have it. Hurry, I don't have much time."

Daggett was terrified. He'd known his health wasn't good. He was always sure he was on the verge of death. But ye gods, this was the first time his diagnosis had been confirmed by Dr. Wiltshire. He wished the doctor had had the good grace to give him the bad news to his face.

Nelda frowned. "You mean your writing box, sir? The gray paisley one?"

He nodded weakly. He had much to get off his conscience. "Get it quickly, girl." He clutched his stomach as a sharp pain speared his lower abdomen. "I've not much time left."

Nelda hurried over to the huge cherrywood armoire, knelt and pulled open the door of the bottom cupboard. Reaching in, she yanked out a large gray-and-gold paisley box. She took it to the bed and laid it next to Mr. Daggett. "Would you like me to change the bed first?"

"There's no time for that now." Wincing as another pain went through him, he forced his big bulk into a sitting position and placed the writing box across his lap. Opening it, he reached inside and took out a pen and piece of paper. "Come back in an hour. I've a very important letter for you to deliver."

"Yes sir." Nelda was a bit puzzled. It wasn't like the master to miss a chance to loll about in clean sheets. But she did as she was bid and left the bedroom, closing the door softly behind her.

Oscar Daggett stared at the blank paper for a moment. One part of him was desperately frightened of what he was about to do, but another part knew he couldn't meet his Maker without confessing. No, he simply couldn't die without telling the truth. Almighty God would never forgive him for staying silent, and he didn't want to spend eternity frying in hell.

And he was dying. He knew it. He'd heard the doctor's grim prognosis with his own ears. Mind you, he was a tad annoyed with his housekeeper for referring to him as an "old stick." That was quite disrespectful. If he wasn't dying and consequently filled with mercy and forgiveness, he might consider sacking the woman for her impertinence.

He took a deep breath, and another sharp pain shot across his chest. He moaned. He'd best get on with it; perhaps he had even less time than he'd thought.

He straightened his spine, put the paper on the lid of the box and positioned the pen in his right hand. He began to write. "For the good of my immortal soul, I, Oscar Daggett do hereby make this confession of my own free will."

He poured out his confession onto the clean, white pages. By the time he'd finished he was exhausted. He slumped against the pillows and closed his eyes, waiting for the end to come.

Precisely one hour later, Nelda came back to his room, knocked and entered slowly. "Sir," she whispered. "Are you asleep?"

"No. Come closer, girl." He motioned for her to come to stand by his bedside. He reached under his pillow and pulled out the letter. "Take this to number thirteen Dunbarton Street," he told her.

"Where's that, sir?" She was a country girl, recently arrived in London. The address meant nothing to her.

"It's in Fulham, girl. Take the letter to number thirteen and give it to the woman that answers the door. Can you remember that?"

"Yes, sir." She took the envelope and stuffed it in the pocket of her stiff white apron. "Do you want me to take it tonight, sir?"

"Right away. Now. Tell me the address again."

Nelda repeated her instructions. She couldn't read very well, but it wasn't much to remember.

"Good. Go now and hurry. I must know that it's been delivered before I pass."

"But what about Mrs. Benchley, sir? She don't allow us out of the house after dark, sir."

"I'm the master here, not Mrs. Benchley. Send her to see me if she tries to stop you. Now, hurry, go on."

"Yes, sir." Nelda bobbed a quick curtsey and hurried out of the room.

Oscar Daggett sighed peacefully and lay back against the pillows. Now that his conscience was clear, he was quite prepared to meet his Maker.

Upon leaving the master's bedroom, Nelda went down to the kitchen to find the household in a tizzy. Mrs. Benchley had fallen in the wet larder and smacked her forehead against the edge of the shelf. The cook and the other maids were gathered around her trying to stanch the flow of the blood.

"Excuse me, Mrs. Benchley," she said. "The master wants me to take a letter to . . ."

"For God's sake, girl, can't you see Mrs. Benchley is busy," the cook scolded. She glared at the impudent housemaid. Stupid country girls. They couldn't see what was right under their noses.

"I'm sorry," Nelda said miserably. "I can see poor Mrs. Benchley is in a terrible state, but Mr. Daggett ordered me to deliver this letter to . . ."

"For goodness' sakes," the cook cried. "Take the wretched letter and be done with it. Do hold still, Mrs. Benchley, we'll have the bleeding stopped in no time."

Nelda gave up trying to explain. Turning, she grabbed her cloak and hat from the rack and hurried out the back door.

"Mrs. Benchley, don't fret so, we'll have you fixed up in just a moment," the cook assured the housekeeper. But Mrs. Benchley didn't answer. Her eyes rolled up in the back of her head, and she slumped back against the chair.

"Oh blast, we'll have to call the doctor," the cook said glumly. "Mr. Daggett won't like that."

"But the bleeding's stopped," Hortense, the tweeny, pointed out. She was standing behind the cook and could only see a portion of the housekeeper's forehead.

"True. But Mrs. Benchley's gone to sleep," the cook replied. "And I don't think that's a good sign. Run along and get Dr. Wiltshire," she ordered the tweeny. "And be sure and tell him it's for Mrs. Benchley and not Mr. Daggett. We want the man to hurry this time."

By the time Dr. Wiltshire arrived, Mrs. Benchley was back in the land of the living. But he was taking no chances. "You have a concussion," he told her. "I don't think it's serious, but with head injuries, one never knows. You must stay in bed for a few days and get plenty of rest."

"Mr. Daggett won't like that, sir," Mrs. Benchley replied. Her head was pounding, and there was a terrible pressure at her temples.

"Not to worry," Dr. Wiltshire assured her, "I'll make it right with Mr. Daggett. He's not a monster, you know; he won't expect you to work when you're ill." He hoped the old boy would see reason, but the fact was, half of his patients were monsters and did expect their servants to do all manner of impossible things, ill or not. Well, dammit, he wasn't going to allow this poor woman to kill herself working. "I'll just pop up and see him." He headed for the back stairs and stopped at the kitchen door. Turning, he addressed the cook. "Have someone help Mrs. Benchley to her room and into bed. Is there someone who can sit with her tonight? She oughtn't to be alone."

The cook hesitated. She wasn't sure what to do. "I suppose Nelda can sit with her." She looked around, wanting to find the girl. "Where is she?"

"Remember, she's gone to deliver a letter," Hortense said helpfully. "She ought to have been back by now. There's a postbox just on the corner."

"Well, go out and have a look for her," the cook ordered. Really, she thought, these country girls were useless. You couldn't depend on them at all. "I'll see that someone sits with Mrs. Benchley," she said to the doctor.

Wiltshire went up to his other patient's room. Daggett was still sitting up in bed, his eyes closed and his hand resting on his protruding stomach. "Egads," he cried, when he caught sight of the doctor, "back so soon. I thought I had another few hours at least."

The doctor was in no mood to put up with Daggett's hysterics. "What are you talking about, man? There's nothing wrong with you but a mild case of indigestion. I told you that this afternoon. Look, your housekeeper's had a bit of an accident . . ."

"I know what you told me," Daggett interrupted. "But I now know the truth. The end is near. The reaper is coming for me. I'm," he paused dramatically, "dying."

Wiltshire wondered if Daggett had ever done a stint on the stage. "Nonsense, Mr. Daggett. You're nowhere near dying. You've got indigestion."

"I'm not dying? Are you sure?" Daggett shot up off the pillows. There was something in the doctor's voice that made him realize he was speaking the truth. "But I heard you talking to my housekeeper. I heard you say there was no hope . . . that the end was near, that it was nature's way and everything had to die."

Wiltshire forced himself to be patient. Daggett wasn't the biggest fool he'd ever dealt with, but he was close. "You overheard me talking to Mrs. Benchley about my orange tree. It's leaves are falling off, and it's dying, not you. Speaking of Mrs. Benchley, I'm afraid she's had an accident. That's why I've come back. She won't be able to work for a few days. I've ordered . . ." He trailed off as he saw Daggett's face go completely white. For once, the fellow actually looked ill. "I say, are you feeling all right?"

Daggett couldn't speak as the enormity of what he'd done hit him full force. He started to get up, but the doctor gently pushed him back. "You don't look at all well. You've gone pale, perhaps I'd better have a look at you . . ."

Daggett shook him off. He had to get that letter back. He had to stop that silly girl from delivering it. "I'm fine," he said. He tossed the bedclothes to one side and swung his legs off the high bed. "Just fine. Not to worry, I'm suddenly feeling fit as a fiddle. I think I'll get dressed and take a bit of air."

Puzzled, the doctor stared at him. "Your color isn't very good, sir. You ought to go back to bed."

"Nonsense." Daggett forced himself to smile. "I'm fine. As you said, it's just a bit of indigestion. Now, what were you saying about Mrs. Benchley?" He barely listened as the doctor detailed the housekeeper's accident. All he could think of was getting to Fulham, to number thirteen Dunbarton Street, and getting that damned letter back.

"Mrs. Benchley must have as much rest as she needs," he muttered when the doctor finished speaking. He hurried over to his armoire and yanked open the top drawer.

"A day or two should do it," Wiltshire replied, watching him closely. The man's behavior was odd, but medically, he now seemed quite all right. His color had returned to normal. "I'll stop by to see Mrs. Benchley tomorrow."

"Good, good," Daggett said. He yanked a pair of clean socks out of the drawer. "Good night, I'll see you tomorrow then." He wished the doctor would hurry and leave. He had to get moving. Oh God, what on earth was he going to do? Whatever had possessed him to write it all down?

The doctor finally left. Daggett threw on his clothes and raced out the bedroom door, almost running into Hortense on the landing. The girl managed to dodge to one side to avoid being run over. "Out of my way, girl. Where's the other one?"

"Other one, sir?" Hortense had no idea what he was talking about. Alarmed, she stared at him. His shirt was hanging out of his trousers, his hair stood straight up, his tie was crooked and the lapel of his jacket was folded in the wrong way.

"The other girl," Daggett shouted. "Where is she?"

"Nelda's not back yet," Hortense replied. She began to back away from him. "I went and looked for her. I went all the way to the postbox at the corner, but I didn't see her. No one's seen her since she left with that letter you give her."

Daggett's eyes almost popped out of his head, then he turned, bolted down the staircase and out the front door.

Harrison Nye sat across from Oscar Daggett and considered killing the man. He carefully weighed the pros and cons of that solution, and then discarded it. Too many people had seen Daggett arrive. How unfortunate that the fool had come blundering in so hysterical he could barely speak when Eliza was having one of her dinner parties.

No, he decided, he couldn't kill him, and that wouldn't solve the problem anyway.

"I didn't know what else to do." Daggett wiped his forehead with his handkerchief. "I can't think what to do."

"Did it occur to you to go to Dunbarton Street and try to get the letter back?" Nye asked.

"That wasn't possible," Daggett said. "The girl had a good two hours' head start on me. I knew it was hopeless. That's why I came here. We've got to decide what to do."

What Nye wanted to do was to wrap his fingers around Daggett's pudgy throat and squeeze the life out of him. "Don't do anything. I'll take care of the matter. You're sure she still lives there?"

Daggett hesitated. "Yes, of course."

But Nye had seen the hesitation. "Damn it, man. You mean there's a chance she isn't there? Tell me the truth now, it's very important. If she got your damned confession, we might be able to deal with the consequences, but if someone else got it, we could be doomed."

"She was living there last summer. I know because I

saw her getting into a hansom on Regent Street. I heard her give the cabbie that Fulham address."

Nye closed his eyes briefly to regain control of himself. He hated losing his temper. It made him do idiotic, impulsive things. But the urge to smack Daggett's fat, stupid face was so strong he had to ball his hand into a fist to keep from hitting him. He'd deal with Daggett later. When he had that letter safely back in his possession. Nye rose to his feet, indicating the meeting was over.

Daggett gaped at him, then lumbered up off the settee as well. "What should I do?"

"Go home," Nye ordered. "Just go home and try to act normal."

"Harrison?" Eliza Nye, a tall, striking redhead in her early thirties, came into the study. "I do hate to interrupt, dear, but we've guests."

"I'm so sorry, sweetheart." Nye smiled at his beautiful wife. She was a good twenty years younger than he. The daughter of minor aristocracy, she'd been the perfect candidate when he'd decided to take a wife. She had breeding, but no money. She was therefore pliable, grateful and willing to overlook his more ruthless character traits. "Let me show Oscar out, then I'll rejoin our guests."

She nodded regally, smiled graciously at Daggett and withdrew.

"You're not going to the house now?" Daggett asked.

"What would be the point?" Nye replied. He started for the door and motioned to Daggett to follow. "She's had time to read it by now. But I doubt she's going to do anything about it until tomorrow. By then, I'll have taken care of the problem once and for all."

They'd reached the hall, and Daggett stopped dead. Behind him, he could hear the sound of the guests through the partially open door of the drawing room. "You're not going to hurt her, are you? I mean . . ." His voice trailed off.

Nye stared at him coldly. "You weren't worried about her welfare fifteen years ago."

"That was different." Daggett swallowed. "What are you going to do?"

"I'm going to take care of our little problem. A problem, I might remind you, that you caused."

"I thought I was dying. I didn't want it on my conscience."

Nye laughed. "We can't have that, can we? Run along home, little man. I'll get that damned letter back, and when I do, I'll be along to see you."

Daggett backed away. Fear curdled in his stomach. "All right, I'll leave it all to you, then." He turned and bolted for the door, almost knocking over a tall, lanky young man who'd just come out of the water closet.

"I say," the young man sputtered apologetically. "Frightfully sorry. I didn't see you . . ." But he was talking to Daggett's back. He turned and looked at his host. "Your friend seems in a deuced hurry. Almost bowled me over."

"Do forgive him, Lionel," Nye said. "He's in a bit of a state. Nervous fellow. You know the sort. Let's go and join the others."

Harrison Nye pulled his heavy overcoat tighter and banged the black-onyx top of his cane against the roof of the hansom. He stuck his head out the side. "Let me off here, if you please."

Obligingly, the cab stopped, and Harrison climbed down onto the wet, cobblestone street. He paid the driver, then waited until the cab turned the corner before he started for his destination. He'd deliberately had the driver drop him here. He was fairly certain she could never be connected with him, but he wasn't taking any chances.

It was past midnight and the October night was cold. A light, misty rain fell. Save for another cab pulling up at a small hotel a little farther up the street, he was completely alone. That's the way he wanted it, no witnesses. Turning, he crossed the road and started for the corner. Dumbarton Street was a long street of small, two-story rowhouses with tiny front gardens. Even in the dark, he could see that most of the houses were unkempt and in need of a good coat of paint.

When he got to the front of number 13, he saw it was in slightly better condition than the others. Nye went up the walkway to the front door. In the distance, he heard the rumble of a train. Reaching in his pocket, he pulled out a small metal object with a thin protruding strip at one end. He stuck it into the lock and turned it gently. But he couldn't hear the small, faint clicks that signaled the opening of the door because that damned train was getting closer. It was so loud now he could barely hear himself think. He tried turning the handle, but the door didn't budge. Damn, he thought, this was supposed to be easy, in and out in a few seconds, just like the old days. No fuss or bother. Why in the hell did she have to live next door to a bloody railway line?

Suddenly, he gasped as a searing pain lanced him from behind. His fingers dropped the lockpick, his arms flailed and he turned to look at his assailant. His eyes widened. "My God, it's you. . . ."

"Where's Betsy?" Smythe, the coachman for Scotland Yard Inspector Gerald Witherspoon, asked as he came into the kitchen. He was a tall, muscular man with dark hair and heavy, rather brutal features. But his true character was reflected in his warm, kind brown eyes and his ready smile.

The housekeeper, Mrs. Jeffries, a short, plump auburn-haired woman in her mid-fifties, pulled out the chair at the head of the table and sat down. "She'll be along directly. I sent her to the station. The inspector forgot his watch, his money clip and his spectacles. He was in a bit of a hurry this morning. But she ought to be back any moment now, she left over two hours ago."

Smythe nodded. "Should I go call Wiggins? He'll need to wash up before he comes to the table. He's covered in filth."

"Yes, thank you; tell him just to wash his hands and face. I'll put a newspaper under his chair to catch the rest of the dirt."

"The lad's worked hard," Mrs. Goodge, the portly, white-haired cook, said as she placed the big brown teapot in front of the housekeeper. "Cleaning them attic rooms is a right old mess. I still think we ought to burn all that old junk instead of having poor Wiggins bring it down to the terrace."

"It is hard work." Mrs. Jeffries picked up the teapot and began to pour. "I told Wiggins he didn't have to do it alone, that we'd get some street lads in to help him, but he was quite adamant he was up to the task."

"Are you going to go through all of it?" the cook asked curiously.

"The inspector wants to see what all is stored up there. He's no idea, you know. From what he learned from his late aunt, most of the stuff in the attic was there when she bought the house. Then, of course, she lived here for a number of years and added to it as well."

"Cor blimey, I've a powerful thirst," Wiggins, an apple-cheeked, brown-haired lad of twenty, announced as he came into the kitchen. He was the household footman. But as the establishment wasn't formal enough to really need a footman, he did any task that needed doing. His face and hands were clean, but his white work shirt and brown trousers were covered in soot.

Mrs. Jeffries got up and grabbed yesterday's *Times* off the pine sideboard. "Don't sit yet," she said, pushing his chair to one side. She put the paper down and motioned for Wiggins to move the chair back onto the newspaper. "There, now you can have your tea in peace without worrying about dirtying the place up."

"Thanks, Mrs. Jeffries," Wiggins replied. Though in truth, he'd not given dirtying the kitchen a moment's thought. He sat down and reached for one of Mrs. Goodge's scones.

"I wish we had a murder," the cook said glumly. "I'm

bored." She was also feeling her age. She knew that her contributions in helping to bringing killers to justice was the most important thing she'd done in her life. She wanted to do a bit more of it while she had the chance.

"What's the 'urry, Mrs. Goodge? It's only been three weeks since our last one," Smythe asked cheerfully.

"That's easy enough for you to say," she replied. "You're young and fit. I'm not so young and not so fit. I want to do my part while I've got the chance."

Mrs. Jeffries frowned in concern. "You're not ill, are you?" It wasn't like the cook to be morbid or self-pitying.

"Of course not, I'm just not as young as I used to be and, frankly, helping the inspector with his cases is a lot more important than what I'm going to be fixing for Tuesday's supper." She waved a hand dismissively. "Don't worry about me, I'm not ready to pick my funeral hymns yet; I just wish we had us a nice murder, that's all." She wished she'd kept her mouth shut. Now all of them would be watching her like hawks, making sure she was all right. But then again, that was the other reason her life was so good now. She had a family. They all did. They had each other.

After a lifetime of living in other people's houses and keeping her distance from the staff lest they not respect her, she'd ended up as cook to Inspector Gerald Witherspoon. No one else would have her because she'd gotten old, but Mrs. Jeffries had hired her. Smythe and Wiggins were already there—they'd both worked for the inspector's Aunt Euphemia and even though the inspector hadn't needed a coachman or a footman, he'd kept them on. Then Betsy, half-starved and frightened to death, had been found on their doorstep and the inspector had hired her as a maid. Then all of a sudden they were investigating murders, helping their dear employer bring killers to justice. Not that he knew about their efforts, of course. That made it even sweeter, she thought. Even more important. Here they were secretly helping to do the most noble thing a person could do and only a handful of people knew the truth. It was exciting, and she wanted to do it as many times as possible before she went to meet her Maker. Indeed she did. But she didn't want the rest of the household thinking she'd gone maudlin in her old age.

"Me too," Wiggins agreed. "I'd much rather be out 'untin' for clues rather than luggin' all that junk down the stairs. The inspector's aunt kept everything, rotten old books, boxes of letters, old bits of cloth."

"Perhaps we ought to let the inspector sort out the papers," Mrs. Jeffries murmured. "Family letters can be very personal. As for the rest, we'll have to ask him what he wants done with the stuff. He may want to give the useful objects to charity."

Smythe glanced at the clock on the sideboard. "Betsy should be back by now, shouldn't she?"

Betsy and Smythe were engaged. He tended to worry about the girl when she wasn't right under his nose. She, being the independent sort, generally ignored him when he was acting too much like a nervous Nellie and did what she pleased. They'd agreed to postpone getting married for the near future. Neither of them was ready to give up their investigating just yet.

"I'm sure she'll be here any minute," Mrs. Jeffries replied. She turned her head toward the window. Like many homes in this part of London, the kitchen was lower than the street level, and one could see the street through the kitchen window. A hansom was pulling up in front of the house. "I believe that's Betsy now."

"Why'd she take a cab?" Mrs. Goodge mused.

"I expect she has a good reason," the housekeeper replied. "Betsy isn't one to waste money."

A few moments later, a pretty, slender blonde wearing a straw bonnet and a blue coat hurried into the kitchen. She was shedding her coat and hat as she walked. "I've got news." She put her things on the coat rack and flew toward the table, eager to share what she'd learned with the others. She slipped into her chair, grabbed Smythe's hand under the table and gave it a squeeze. "We've got us a murder."

"Ask and thou shalt receive." Mrs. Goodge rolled her eyes heavenward. "Thank you, Lord."

"Who was killed?" Mrs. Jeffries asked.

"A man named Harrison Nye," Betsy said. She accepted the cup of tea the housekeeper handed her. "He was found stabbed to death in a garden in Fulham."

"Whose garden?" Mrs. Goodge asked. She liked to get as many details as possible. As she did all her investigating right from this kitchen, it was important to get as many names as possible as quickly as possible. Mrs. Goodge had a secret army of informants. Deliverymen, rags-and-bones boys, chimney sweeps, gas men, 'tweenys and street arabs. She plied them with tea and cake and got their tongues wagging. If that didn't work, she used her vast network of former colleagues, which stretched from one end of London to the other, to unearth every morsel of gossip about suspects and victims. She could do a better background investigation on someone than the spies at the foreign office and do it quicker as well.

Betsy took a quick sip of tea. "I don't know. I only got the name of the victim and the address. It was number thirteen Dunbarton Street in Fulham. That's where he was found."

"Harrison Nye," Smythe repeated thoughtfully. "That name sounds familiar. Now where 'ave I 'eard it before?"

"Tell us what happened," Mrs. Jeffries said to Betsy. It was important that they get the full story. She knew that it was easy to leave out something that could be a vital clue when one was telling something piecemeal.

"I got to the station and the sergeant on duty let me go up to the inspector's office. He wasn't there. He was in a meeting of some sort, so I put his things on his desk. Then I left to come home, but just as I was leaving the building, who should pop up but Inspector Nivens."

Everyone groaned. Inspector Nigel Nivens was universally and heartily disliked. The man had made it his mission in life to prove that Inspector Witherspoon had help solving his cases. He was rude, caustic and quite stupid.

"That was my reaction as well," Betsy said with a grin. She'd groaned when he'd waylaid her in the foyer. "But as it turned out, it was just as well. If Nivens hadn't stopped me, I wouldn't have found out about the inspector nor the name of the victim."

"What happened?" Mrs. Goodge asked.

Betsy's grin broadened. "Well, there I was trying to get away from Nivens, who was asking me what I was doing there in the first place, when all of a sudden, who should come racing down the stairs but our inspector and Constable Barnes. He stopped when he saw me, thanked me for bringing his things, then told me to tell you"—she nodded at Mrs. Jeffries—"that he'd be home quite late tonight as he'd just been given a murder. You should have seen Inspector Nivens's face. He got so angry he looked like he was going to have an apoplexy attack. He demanded to know who'd been killed and where it had happened. Of course our inspector told him, and that's how I heard. Then Nivens took off up the stairs muttering something to the effect that this should be his murder and that the chief inspector had no business giving it to our inspector." She broke off and laughed. "Oh, you should have seen him. It was a sight. Even the police constables milling about and the sergeant were staring at Nivens like he'd lost his mind."

"Nye. That name sounds so familiar," Smythe muttered again.

Betsy was glad her beloved was so worried about who the victim was rather than why Nivens had stopped her in the first place. She'd told them he'd been questioning her about why she was at the station and that, to some extent, was the truth. He'd whipped off his hat, done a funny little bow and then grinned at her like she ought to be grateful he was taking any notice of her at all. It had taken a few minutes before she'd realized he was flirting with her. She'd been horrified. He'd actually had the nerve to ask her when was her day out.

She'd told him her day out each week varied according to what the household's needs happened to be. Mercifully, the inspector and Constable Barnes had come rushing down the stairs at that point.

The inspector hadn't noticed anything amiss with her, but she'd seen the constable's eyes narrow suspiciously. Constable Barnes didn't miss much. She'd seen him shoot Nivens a really dirty look too.

She had no intention of seeing Nigel Nivens on her day out, and she'd tell him so the next time she saw him. She couldn't stand the little toad, and she was an engaged woman. She intended to keep it that way.

"Should we send for Luty and Hatchet?" Mrs. Goodge asked.

Luty Belle Crookshank and her butler Hatchet were dear friends. They'd inadvertently gotten involved in one of the inspector's earlier cases and ended up using their considerable resources to help catch a killer. Now they helped all the time.

"I can pop along and get 'em," Wiggins volunteered. "If they're 'ome, I can 'ave 'em back 'ere before noon."

"That'd give me time to nip around to Fulham and see what I can suss out about the murder," Smythe said. "Cor blimey, though, I wish I could remember where I'd heard that name."

"Do be careful, Smythe," Mrs. Jeffries cautioned. "If Nivens is on his high horse, he could well be snooping around number thirteen Dunbarton Street even if it isn't his case."

"I'll keep my eyes open, Mrs. Jeffries," Smythe said. "But we need to get crackin'. It's not often we get a jump on a case like this."

CHAPTER 2

"The doctor is finished, sir," Constable Barnes said to the inspector. "We'd better have a look. The van to take him to the mortuary will be here any moment now."

The doctor, a portly, balding fellow with a huge handlebar mustache, rose from where he'd been kneeling beside the body and started toward the waiting policemen. "I'm Dr. John Boyer," he introduced himself as he drew near.

Witherspoon extended his hand, and the two men shook. "I'm Inspector Gerald Witherspoon and this is Constable Barnes. What can you tell us, Doctor?"

Boyer nodded at the constable. "Not much at this stage," he replied. "Fellow's been stabbed. But I'm not saying that's the cause of death. I won't know that officially until I do the postmortem."

"When will you be finished with the autopsy?" he asked. From the corner of his eye, he could see that quite a crowd of locals had gathered. Several police constables were keeping them well away from the crime scene.

"I'll do it this morning and get the report over to you

straight away." Boyer smiled slightly. "Providing, of course, that I don't have any emergencies waiting for me when I get to my office. Now, gentlemen, if you'll excuse me, I must be off. Oh, by the way, you might want to have your lads do a search of the local area. From the size of the wound, my guess, and mind you, it's only a guess at this stage, is that he was killed with a fairly large knife." He nodded one last time and turned on his heel and left.

"That's not good, sir." Constable Barnes pursed his lips. "It's better if we've got the murder weapon."

"I agree," Witherspoon replied. He began walking toward the corpse. "But we don't. As soon as we examine the body, we'd best do as the doctor says and have our lads do a thorough search. Most killers try to rid themselves of the weapon as soon as possible." He turned his head and looked off to where the road ended. Beyond the last house, there was a spindly copse of trees. The Fulham and Putney Railway line was just the other side of the trees. "Have them search amongst the trees."

"How about the railway line? How far should they walk it in each direction?" He started toward the body.

Witherspoon followed. He'd solved many murders, yet sometimes the simplest question caught him off guard. "Uh, well, I'm not sure."

"I'll have them go a mile each way, sir." Barnes reached the victim first. He knelt beside the body. "It's pretty bad, sir," he said. "There's a lot of blood. Looks like the knife went straight in through his back to the heart. Must have hurt like the devil too."

Witherspoon hung back for a few moments, then took a deep breath and stepped to the other side of the dead man. He knew his duty. He hoped he wouldn't disgrace himself by getting sick. Stabbing victims, in particular, always made him queasy. Mindful of the crowd eagerly watching from the sidelines, he forced himself to look down at the corpse sprawled at his feet.

The victim lay on his side, his body half on and half

off the stone walkway leading to the front door of the small house. Blood seeped out from underneath the man's back and pooled thinly on the stone. He'd worn a black overcoat, and it was soaked through of course. The inspector noted the position of the fatal wound and looked at Barnes. "Let's roll him over," he instructed. He knelt, took a deep breath and grasped the dead man's shoulder. He and the constable turned him onto his back.

The corpse's eyes were wide-open. "I say, he does look rather surprised," Witherspoon murmured. "But then again, being stabbed in the back is rather unexpected."

"Should we search his pockets, sir?"

"Good idea," Witherspoon replied. He reached into the overcoat and his fingers brushed against its silk lining. He felt around the inside pocket thoroughly. "Nothing in here."

Barnes had plunged his hands into the trouser pockets. "Just what you'd expect, sir," he said. "A money clip loaded with small bills and some coins. Nothing else."

"How was he identified so quickly?" Witherspoon asked.

Barnes jerked his chin toward one of the police constables standing at the edge of the front garden holding the crowd back. "Constable Peters recognized him, sir. He moved him enough to get a good look at his face before he raised the alarm, sir. He said he wanted to make sure the fellow was dead."

Witherspoon nodded. "I'll have a word with him in a moment." He rose to his feet and stared at the silent house in front of them. Then he looked at the crowd being held back by the police constables. "Who lives here?" he called to the nearest constable.

"No one," he replied. "The house has been empty for over two months."

As the small crowd had gone quiet and was now avidly listening, Witherspoon decided it might be best to ask his questions more discreetly. "Thank you, Constable."

"I'll have a quiet word with the local lads, sir," Barnes said. "They'll be able to give us a few more details about this place." He had realized the inspector's dilemma. The police wanted information, but they didn't want the entire neighborhood to watch them getting it.

"Which one of you is Constable Peters?" Witherspoon called out.

"I am, sir." A tall young man with dark brown hair detached himself from the others and came to the inspector. The lad's face was pasty white, and the expression in his hazel eyes haunted.

"Is this your first body?" the inspector asked softly.

Peters nodded. "Yes, sir. And to tell you the truth, I hope it'll be my last. It weren't pleasant, sir. Not pleasant at all." In truth, Constable Peters had almost lost his stomach, but he wasn't about to share that with the legendary Inspector Gerald Witherspoon. Mind you, Peters thought, the inspector didn't look much like a legend. His face was long and kind of bony. Wisps of thin brown hair fluttered from underneath his bowler, and his spectacles had slipped halfway down his nose. No, Peters decided, he didn't look like a legend at all. More like a mustached little mouse of a man. Except for the spectacles, of course. Mice didn't wear spectacles . . .

"Constable Peters, are you all right?" Witherspoon asked sharply.

"Sorry, sir." Peters realized the inspector had asked him a question. "What did you say?"

"Who found the body?" Witherspoon repeated for the second time. Goodness, the poor lad really was rattled.

"A Mrs. Moff. She lives next door."

A police van trundled around the corner, and there was a flurry of activity as the constables holding the crowd back shooed people out of the way so the van could draw up close to the house.

"The wagon's here, sir," Barnes said. "Did you want to have another look at the body before they take it off, sir?"

"No. Let's go have a word with this Mrs. Moff, then," the inspector said.

"Are you finished with me, sir?" Peters asked.

"Not quite, Constable," Witherspoon replied. "There's a café up the road a bit. Go and have a cup of tea, a nice strong one with lots of sugar. As soon as Constable Barnes and I are finished here, we'll be along to get a few more details from you."

Constable Peters hesitated. He was suddenly ashamed of himself for thinking Inspector Witherspoon looked like a mouse. Blooming Ada, the man must be able to read minds, he'd just been thinking he'd give a week's pay for a cuppa. But he didn't want the others to think him a ninny. "I'm all right, sir . . ."

"Go along, lad," Barnes said brusquely. He understood the young man didn't want to appear weak. "Do as the inspector says and have a cup of tea. No one will think any the less of you for it." They moved to one side as two police constables, a stretcher slung between them, hurried up the short walkway to the victim.

Peters, with one last terrified glance over his shoulder at the dead man, muttered a quick thanks to his superiors and took off down the road like a shot. Apparently, watching the victim get hauled away was more than he could stomach.

Barnes watched the police constables in their grim task long enough to ascertain that they knew what they were doing. Then he and the inspector made their way next door.

Witherspoon raised his hand to knock just as the door flew open. A middle-aged woman with a long nose and a flat, disapproving slash of a mouth stuck her head out and glared at them. "It took you long enough. That fellow's been dead for hours."

"I'm sorry, madam." Witherspoon was a bit taken aback. "We got here as quickly as possible."

"Humph," she snorted, and motioned them inside. "Come in, then, and let's get this over with. This whole business has upset my day enough already and I need to get to the shops before they close."

They stepped into a dim, narrow hallway. The walls were painted a pale yellow that hadn't aged particularly well and the air was heavy with the scent of wet wool and stale beer.

The inspector waited until the lady of the house had closed the door. She gave them a disgruntled look as she brushed past them. "Get a move on, then, I've told you, I've not got all day."

"I'm Inspector Witherspoon, and this is Constable Barnes," the inspector said as they trailed behind her. She grunted in response and turned to her left into an open doorway.

They followed her into a neatly furnished small sitting room. White antimacassars were placed on the backs of the sagging gray settee and chairs. The table by the window was covered with a fringed shawl and a spindly-looking fern was doing its best to soak up what little sun it could through the pale muslin curtains.

"I'm Mrs. Moff." She sat down smack in the middle of the couch and looked pointedly at the two chairs.

Witherspoon and Barnes each took a seat. The inspector waited until Barnes whipped out his little brown notebook and his pencil, then he said, "I understand you're the one who found the body."

"Right." Mrs. Moff bobbed her head up and down as she spoke. "I did. Saw him lying there big as you please when I went out this morning."

"What time was that, ma'am?" the constable asked.

"Oh, it was right early. The sun were just comin' up when I stepped outside and saw him lying there. I went dashing over to see what was what, but when I was a few feet away, I saw the blood and I knew he was done for. So I went off and got the copper on the corner."

"Constable Peters," Barnes said to Witherspoon. "This is his patch."

"Right, I see him every morning on my way to the

baker's. Mr. Moff and I get us a couple of buns every morning for our breakfast." Mrs. Moff's head began bobbing again. "I got the constable, and we come back here. He took one look at the fellow and gave a mighty blast on that whistle of his and before you could count your linens, there were more coppers about the place than fleas on a dog. Well, I told the constable what little I knew, went on and got my buns and come back inside. Mr. Moff and I had our breakfast, and he went off to work. I've been waiting for you ever since."

Witherspoon stared at her for a moment. She certainly wasn't upset that a murder had taken place right under her nose, so to speak. "Did Mr. Moff see the body?"

Mrs. Moff's thick eyebrows rose in surprise. "No, why should he? He's seen dead uns before."

"Really?" Witherspoon said.

"Course he has," Mrs. Moff said staunchly. "He works over at Fulham Cemetery, has done for nigh onto twenty-two years now. You know, digging graves and that sort of thing. Mind you, they're usually in the box by the time Mr. Moff has anything to do with 'em, but not always. No, no, seein' a dead body wasn't something Mr. Moff wanted to do before he'd even had his buns."

"Er, did you happen to hear anything unusual during the night?" Witherspoon asked.

"Unusual?" She seemed puzzled by the question.

"You know," Constable Barnes interjected, "did you hear footsteps or screaming or anything that might have been just a bit out of the ordinary?" He tried to keep the sarcasm out of his tone but wasn't quite successful.

Mrs. Moff appeared not to notice. "You mean did I hear the killing? No, slept like a log, I did. Now Mr. Moff's a light sleeper. He might have heard something."

"What time will Mr. Moff be home?" the inspector asked quickly.

"Half past six," she replied proudly. "Regular as clockwork, he is. Why? Do you want to speak to him?"

"That's the idea," the inspector replied. He knew there

were a number of other questions he ought to ask, but for
the life of him, his mind had gone blank.

"Who owns the house next door?" Constable Barnes
asked.

"Which one?"

Barnes took a deep breath. He'd met stupider people.
He was sure of it, but he couldn't remember when. "The
one where the murder happened."

"Oh, that one." She nodded wisely. "Well, as far as I
know, Miss Geddy still owns the place. Mind you, I can't
say it for a fact, she might have sold it, because she just
up and disappeared one day without so much as a by-
your-leave. She didn't say a word about where she was
goin' or if she'd be back. The house 'as been empty ever
since."

The two men looked at each other. Then Witherspoon
leaned forward slightly. "What is Miss Geddy's first
name? What can you tell me about her?"

"Why do you want to know?" Mrs. Moff frowned. "I
just told you, Miss Geddy's been gone for nigh on to two
months now. What could she have to do with this killing?"

Barnes opened his mouth to speak, but the inspector
beat him to it. "Probably nothing, ma'am. But it's important we know as much as possible. Now, please, just answer the question."

"It's all the same to me," Mrs. Moff said with a shrug.
"Her name's Frieda Geddy, and she come here about fifteen years ago. That's all I know about the woman."

Barnes looked up from his notebook. "How long have
you lived here?"

"Twenty years." Her eyes narrowed. "Why? What do
you care how long I've been here?"

"As you implied you knew very little about your neighbor, I wondered if you'd just moved here," he replied.

"I don't know much about her because she kept to herself," Mrs. Moff shot back. "And I mind my own business, too. There, that satisfy you?"

"Has Miss Geddy any relatives in the area?" Wither-spoon asked quickly.

"How would I know?" Mrs. Moff sniffed disapprov-ingly. "I just told you, she weren't one to get friendly."

"Did she have any visitors?" he persisted. Even if she did mind her own business, she had eyes. She could have seen someone coming and going next door.

Mrs. Moff's expression darkened. "I don't know, In-spector. I didn't spend my time watchin' her, and I don't know why you're goin' on and on about some toff-nosed woman that's been gone for over two months now. What's she got to do with anything? She ain't the one lying out there dead now, is she?"

Smythe hovered on the corner of Dunbarton Street and Hurlingham Road. He didn't dare get any closer to the house, he didn't want to be seen. But by keeping his ears open, he'd learned a lot. For starters, he'd found out the victim wasn't a local man.

"What's goin' on?" he said casually to a young lad who'd come out of one of the houses on the other side of Dunbarton Street.

The sandy-haired lad of about fourteen stopped in his tracks. "Fellow's been murdered. Bloke got stabbed in Miss Geddy's front garden. The body's in that van"—he pointed to the police van—"and they're fixing to take it away."

"Murder." Smythe shook his head. "That's awful. 'Ave they caught who done it?"

"Nah, they'll not catch him." The boy shrugged. "This'll be like that Ripper murder. They'll never catch who did it." His eyes sparkled with excitement as he spoke. "Mind you, my mam thinks it must be the same person who done in Miss Geddy."

"Miss Geddy? You mean someone else 'as been killed?"

"They ain't never found her body," the lad explained, "but she disappeared. Ain't been seen for over two months. And now look what's happened. Some bloke gets himself sliced up in her front garden."

"Harold, what are you doin'? You get on to the chemist's now and quit larking about," a woman's voice screeched at the hapless boy from the window of the house behind them. "I need my Bexley's Pills, I've got a bleedin' headache."

The boy rolled his eyes and sighed, but turned toward the corner.

Smythe hesitated for a split second. He had a feeling he oughn't to let the lad get away from him. This "disappearance" might not be connected to the murder at all, but then again, it might. He fell into step beside Harold. "So this 'ere Miss Geddy disappeared too, you say?"

"One day she was there, the next day she weren't."

They rounded the corner and headed up the road toward the shops. Harold, delighted to have an audience, kept on chatting a mile a minute. "Mind you, me mam says we don't none of us know how long it were before we even noticed Miss Geddy were gone, kept herself to herself, she did. But she's gone, and that's a fact."

They'd reached the shops. "I've got to get me mam's medicine," Harold said.

Smythe racked his brain trying to think of something he needed. "Oh, I need to pop in and get a bottle of liniment for our housekeeper." He pulled the door open, and the two of them went inside.

They made their purchases in just a few minutes and stepped back into the weak autumn sunshine. Smythe had a few more questions to ask the lad. He looked at him speculatively. "I'm goin' over to that café"—he nodded toward a workingman's café a few doors up—"and havin' a cup of tea and a bun. You're welcome to come along."

Harold's eyes narrowed suspiciously.

"Truth is," Smythe continued quickly, "I work for a detective . . ."

"You mean one of them private inquiry agents?" Harold interrupted excitedly.

"In a way," Smythe hedged. He hated to out and out lie to the boy. But he wanted to talk to him. Not only could the lad tell him about this mysterious disappearance, but he'd probably know a number of details about the murder. Young lads like him were natural snoops, and this Harold looked like a bright young chap. "We're workin' on a case. A case that might involve your Miss Geddy and this 'ere dead bloke in 'er front garden."

Harold nodded eagerly and started down the road. "I'll just run Mam's medicine home, then I'll meet ya at the café. Will ya buy me a bun?"

"I'll buy ya more than one if you've a hunger," Smythe promised. Grinning, he watched the boy run around the corner. But his smile abruptly faded as, a moment later, he spotted Constable Barnes and the inspector heading his way. "Cor blimey," he muttered. "What's he doin'?"

Smythe turned on his heel and took off toward the corner. If he was lucky, he could duck into the café without being spotted.

His long legs ate up the short distance in no time. He yanked open the door and stepped inside. His eyes widened as he saw a police constable sitting at a table near the back of the café. Blast a Spaniard, he thought, what's he doing here? Smythe had worked for the inspector long enough to know that police constables didn't sit around drinking tea when a murder had been committed. They were out searching for murder weapons and taking statements and doing house-to-house searches. They blooming weren't sitting around on their backsides drinking tea.

As unobtrusively as possible, Smythe eased out the door, spun on his heel and sauntered off. The inspector and Barnes were less than fifty yards away. But they were so engrossed in their conversation, they didn't notice him.

He hunched his shoulders as he skirted the traffic, waiting for a break between the hansoms, wagons and horses so he could dash across the road. Finally, he loped across and reached the safety of the other side. He winced as he thought of poor Harold. He hoped the lad wouldn't be too disappointed not to get his buns. Smythe dodged around a costermonger pushing a handcart of jellied eels. He'd find the lad tomorrow and do his best to make it up to him.

Constable Barnes squinted at the broad back and the hunched shoulders of the big bloke walking ahead of them. There was something very familiar about the fellow.

"I do think it'll be worth coming back and interviewing Mr. Moff," the inspector said. "He may have heard something."

"Right, sir. Perhaps we can come back this evening."

"That's a good idea, Constable." They'd reached the café. Witherspoon pulled the door open and they stepped inside. A short, red-faced fellow wearing a dirty apron stood behind the counter. There were five small tables scattered around the room and a long counter down one wall. The scent of hot tea and fried eggs filled the air. Except for one table where Constable Peters was sitting, the place was deserted. Constable Peters, seeing them, rose to his feet.

Witherspoon waved him back to his seat. "Would you be so kind as to get us both some tea, Constable Barnes."

"Certainly, sir." Barnes headed for the counter, and the inspector went and sat down opposite Peters. He noticed the man wasn't quite as pale as he'd been. "You look a lot better than you did earlier."

Peters smiled gratefully. "I feel better, sir. I'm sorry, I mean, I didn't mean to get all het up . . . it's just I've never seen someone who's been murdered."

"There's no need to apologize," the inspector said quickly. "I understand. I'd like to say it gets easier over time, but the truth is, it doesn't. Death is bad enough, no one but an undertaker could ever get used to it, but murder is quite different. It's shocking and obscene. I hope to God none of us ever get used to it."

"Here we are, sir." Barnes put two steaming cups of milky tea on the small table and sat down.

"Thank you, Constable," Witherspoon said. "Now, Constable Peters, tell us how you happened to be able to identify the victim so quickly."

"I've seen him before, sir. Lots of times. He lives on Belgravia Square on Upper Belgrave Street. That was my patch when I first joined the force. I used to see Mr. Nye every morning as I was walking my beat."

Witherspoon nodded approvingly. "You'd met him, then?"

"Yes, sir. He was a pleasant enough fellow. Always nodded and spoke when he walked past. I was called to a disturbance at his house right before I was transferred here. Someone had tossed a brick through one of his windows."

"Tossed a brick through his window?" Witherspoon repeated. "How very odd. Was it a robbery?"

"No sir. Someone just chucked a ruddy huge brick through Mr. Nye's front window, then went running off. It was done in the middle of the night, sir. We'd not a hope of catching 'em." Peters gave an embarrassed shrug. "Mr. Nye was rather annoyed. He said we weren't doing our job properly. I think he might have filed a complaint, sir. He was really angry about that window. I was surprised a bit, I mean, like I said, he always seemed a pleasant enough sort."

Witherspoon said nothing. He wasn't sure what to make of this. But then again, perhaps it had nothing to do with Mr. Nye's demise. Random cases of vandalism weren't unheard of, even in the better parts of London.

"How long ago did this happen?" Barnes asked.

Peter's brow creased as he thought back. "Let me see, now. It was a few days before I moved over here, and I've been walking this beat for about two months."

"Two months." The inspector frowned and glanced at Barnes. "Didn't Miss Moff say that Miss Geddy had been missing for about two months?"

"That's what she said, sir. But we don't really know that the woman is missing."

"The neighbors have all talked about Miss Geddy being missing," Peters interjected, "but no one has filed a report, sir. So we've not investigated." He blushed as they looked at him. "Sorry, I didn't mean to interrupt your discussion."

"That's quite all right," Witherspoon said quickly. "We need all the information we can get. So let me see, no one's filed a report so officially, Miss Geddy isn't missing."

"That's right, sir," Peters agreed. "She just hasn't been seen by her neighbors in that time, and now there's been a murder in her front garden."

Witherspoon sighed. He knew this case was going to get complicated. He just knew it. "All right, then, we'll deal with the missing Miss Geddy later. Right now, we've got to get this murder investigation under way. What is Mr. Nye's address? We really must let his family know what's happened as soon as possible."

"What's taking everyone so long?" Mrs. Goodge asked as she put a plate of scones on the table. "We've got to get cracking on this case."

"I'm sure someone will be back soon," Mrs. Jeffries said calmly. "Luty and Hatchet might not be at home."

"Let's hope Wiggins can track them down, then," Mrs. Goodge muttered. "They hate being left out."

Mrs. Jeffries cocked her head toward the street. "I believe I hear a carriage pulling up as we speak."

"That's them," Betsy said as she came into the kitchen.

"Where's Smythe got to, then?" the cook complained. "He should have been back by now."

"Fulham isn't just around the corner," Betsy said defensively. "It'll take him a bit of time to get there and back. Plus, he's got to be able to nose about a bit. Otherwise, there was no point in him going."

They heard the clatter of footsteps and the babble of voices from the back hallway.

"Howdy everyone." The voice was loud, brash and American. It came from the mouth of an elderly, white-haired woman dressed in a bright blue dress. She had on a huge matching bonnet dripping with lace and ribbon.

Directly behind her came a tall, dignified gentleman with white hair. He wore an old-fashioned black frock coat and a pristine white shirt with a high collar. In one hand he carried his black top hat and in the other, he had an ebony cane.

Wiggins trailed in last. Fred, their mongrel dog, leapt up from his spot by the footman's chair and bounded out to meet them. He gave Luty and Hatchet a perfunctory tail wag and bounded over to the footman. "There's a good boy," Wiggins crooned to the dog.

Everyone greeted the new arrivals. Luty Belle Crookshank and her butler, Hatchet, were not just friends, they were as much a part of the inspector's cases as the others. They took their places at the table.

"Should we wait for Smythe?" Betsy asked. She was as eager as the rest of them to get started, but she didn't want to be disloyal to her intended, either. Mind you, she did think it a tad unfair that he was already out and about.

"We'll give him a few moments," Mrs. Jeffries said. "Why don't you tell them what happened when you took the inspector's things to the station."

Betsy told them how she'd heard the news about the murdered man.

"Harrison Nye?" Hatchet frowned thoughtfully. "That name sounds very familiar."

"That's what Smythe said," Wiggins interjected. He paused as they heard the sound of the back door opening and then footsteps coming down the hall.

"Sorry I'm late." Smythe bounded into the kitchen. He paused by the sideboard long enough to lay down the small, paper-wrapped parcel containing the liniment he'd bought at the chemist's. He hoped Mrs. Goodge could use the stuff. He smiled at Betsy first then the others. "But I've 'ad more than my fair share of aggravation this mornin'." He pulled out his chair and plopped down.

"This ought to help, then." Betsy handed him a cup of

tea. "I've just finished telling Luty and Hatchet how I heard we'd a murder. We've been waiting for you, I hope you've plenty to tell us."

Smythe took a quick sip. In truth, he was parched. He felt like he'd run all over blooming London. "You're goin' to be disappointed, then, because I didn't find out much at all. The bloke was murdered, all right. Stabbed in the back. Odd thing is, he wasn't a local. As a matter of fact, the house where he was killed is empty and has been empty for two months."

"Have you remembered where you'd heard his name before?" Mrs. Goodge asked. "Hatchet seemed to feel it sounded familiar to him too."

Smythe shook his head. "No, for the life of me, I just can't remember . . . but I know I've heard it." He glanced at Hatchet. "Where'd you hear it?"

"Unfortunately, I'm in the same quandary as you. I simply can't recall." He shook his head. "It's rather annoying not to be able to bring it to mind . . ."

"The harder you try to remember, the worse it'll get," Luty said. "Just set it aside, both of you. When you're not thinking about who this feller is, that's when it'll come to one of you." She directed her gaze to Smythe. "So this Nye fellow was stabbed in a deserted house?"

"On the walkway," Smythe explained. "I saw the body. It looked to me like the man must have been right at the front door when he got knifed." He glanced at Betsy to make sure she wasn't offended by his rather colorful description, but she was listening as hard as the rest of them.

"What do you mean?" Mrs. Jeffries asked. She didn't doubt the importance of the coachman's observations, she merely wanted more details as to how he'd come by them.

Smythe reached for a bun. "Well, I got there before the mortuary van arrived, and I saw the body before they had a chance to muck it about. It was lying just this side of the front door, on his side, he was. It looked to me like someone had come up behind him and knifed him just as he reached the front door."

"But didn't you just say the house was deserted?" Luty asked.

"That's what don't make sense." Smythe popped a bite of bun in his mouth. "Why would anyone be visiting an empty house in the middle of the night?"

"Why do you think he was killed in the middle of the night?" Luty asked.

"I don't know when he was killed, but I overheard one of the neighbors sayin' as he weren't lyin' there at eleven last night because her husband come home late and he'd have noticed a bloody great corpse in the neighbor's front garden. If she were tellin' the truth, that would mean he had to 'ave been killed later that night."

"Or early this morning," Luty said.

"Whose house is it?" Betsy asked. "Maybe it belongs to this Nye fellow, and that's why he was there so late at night."

"That's another interestin' bit," Smythe said. "It belongs to a woman named Miss Geddy. Seems she up and disappeared herself about two months ago. Some of the locals think she's been murdered."

"You mean we've got two murders?" Wiggins exclaimed.

"I don't know what we've got." Smythe took another fast sip of tea. "I didn't get a chance to find out more. I was going to meet this lad at the corner café and see what he knew about everything, when blow me for a tin soldier, if I don't see the inspector and Constable Barnes coming straight at me."

"They didn't see you, did they?" Mrs. Jeffries asked.

"I don't think so," he replied. "But it were a close call. I thought I'd go back to the neighborhood this afternoon and have another go at sussin' out what's what."

Mrs. Jeffries thought about it for a moment. They didn't know much. But they did have some names and the address where the murder took place. That was enough to start with. "I think that's a very good idea. As a matter of fact, I think we should all get out and see what we can learn."

"I can git over to the city and see what I can find out about this Harrison Nye fellow," Luty said eagerly. "You always say we ought to start with the victim."

"That's an excellent idea, Luty," Mrs. Jeffries replied. If the murdered man had so much as a farthing invested with anyone in the City of London, Luty would get the details.

"I do wish I could remember where I'd heard that name," Hatchet muttered. "Never mind, then, I've a few resouces of my own to tap. Should I see if anyone has heard of this Miss Geddy?"

"Get all the information you can find," Mrs. Jeffries replied. She glanced at Betsy. "Would you mind going over to Fulham and having a go at the shopkeepers?"

Betsy grinned. "I was planning on it. Too bad this Nye fellow wasn't a local. Maybe I ought to concentrate on finding out about this Miss Geddy . . ."

"You'd best be careful, there's going to be police all over Hurlingham Road. That's where all the shops are. A good many of them know you by sight."

Betsy shrugged. "I'll be careful."

"We'll go together, then," Smythe said. He looked at Mrs. Jeffries. "Will you be here this afternoon?"

Mrs. Jeffries thought about it for a moment. She glanced at Mrs. Goodge. The cook's eyes were sparkling with excitement, and there was a half-formed smile on her lips. Mrs. Jeffries was greatly relieved. This murder really had perked up the cook. "I'm going to do the shopping. I'm sure we're in need of a few things."

"Good. That'll help," Mrs. Goodge said. "I know we're a few days early and we could have made do with what we've got, but if I'm going to feed my sources, I'm going to need provisions right away. I'll give you a list of what I want—oh yes, and could you stop at the greengrocer's and get some apples? Those turnovers Lady Cannonberry gave me the recipe for are very popular. People chat their heads off when I've a plate of those on the table."

That was precisely why Mrs. Jeffries had decided to do the shopping. She knew that Mrs. Goodge had been battling a bit of melancholia lately. This murder had come along at just the right time. She didn't want anything interfering with the cook's enthusiasm for pursuing justice. "Of course. I had a quick look in the dry larder this morning. We seem to be low on a number of things. We can't have that. Your sources expect to be fed."

CHAPTER 3

———◆◆◆◆———

"Looks as if Mr. Nye was doin' all right for himself,"
Constable Barnes muttered. He and the Inspector stood on
the doorstep of a huge town house on Upper Belgrave
Street, right off Belgravia Square. The neighborhood was
rich, and so was the victim's house. The door was freshly
painted, and the brass post lamps and knocker were polished to a high shine. "On the other hand, as I've learned
from you, sir, appearances can be very deceiving."

Witherspoon nodded. "Indeed they can, Constable. I
say, this is the very worst part of the job, isn't it?"

Barnes nodded and reached for the knocker. "Telling
the family is always hard, sir." He banged it once and
stepped back.

After a few moments, the door opened, and a butler
appeared. His eyes widened slightly as his gaze took in
Constable Barnes's uniform. "Oh dear, you are quick. We
only just sent for you."

"Sent for us?" Witherspoon repeated.

"Indeed," the butler said. He opened the door wider and
waved them inside. "The footman isn't even back yet."

"Is that the police?" A woman's voice came from above them.

They stepped inside and stared up the curving staircase from where the voice had come.

"Yes, madam, it is." The butler looked very confused. "But I don't quite understand. We've only just sent for them, and Angus isn't even back yet."

"That doesn't matter," she said. "They're here."

Witherspoon glanced at Barnes as a tall, rather lovely auburn-haired young woman flew down the stairway.

"Have you found my husband?" she asked. Her eyes were frantic with worry. "Is he all right? Is he ill?"

Witherspoon sighed inwardly as he realized what had happened. They'd sent for the police this morning when they'd realized that Mr. Nye hadn't come home last night. Drat. "Are you Mrs. Harrison Nye?" he asked gently.

"Yes," she nodded. "I'm Eliza Nye. Where's my husband?"

"Mrs. Nye," the inspector said softly. "Is there anyone here with you?"

"Just the servants." Her brows drew together in confusion. "Oh good Lord, what's wrong? Where's my husband?"

Constable Barnes looked at the butler. "Do you have a housekeeper?" At the man's nod, he continued, "Then get her, quickly. We're going to take Mrs. Nye into the drawing room. Have her join us there and ask the maid to bring some tea."

Uncertain about taking orders from a stranger, the butler hesitated for a brief second, then realized something was terribly wrong and that these two policemen weren't here to give them good news. He gulped audibly and hurried off.

"I think you'd better sit down." The inspector took her arm. "Let's go into the drawing room, madam. I'm afraid I've some very bad news."

The color drained out of her face. But she said nothing. She took a deep breath and led the way across the foyer.

They went through a set of double doors and into a beautifully furnished drawing room. Done in creams and gold, there were settees and overstuffed chairs, fringed shawls on the tables, brass sconces on the walls, and a floor polished to a high gloss. But the inspector barely took in the lavish furnishings. His attention was completely on the young woman who stared at him with huge, beseeching eyes. She looked positively terrified.

But to her credit, she didn't give in to the fear so evident on her face. "Something terrible has happened, hasn't it?"

"I'm afraid so," Witherspoon said. He saw the housekeeper come into the room and make her way toward them.

"It's my husband, isn't it? He's hurt."

"It's a bit worse than that. I'm dreadfully sorry, Mrs. Nye, but your husband was found dead this morning in Fulham."

She stared at them for a moment, her expression more puzzled than shocked. "Dead? But that's ridiculous. Why would he be in Fulham?"

"We don't know why he was there, Mrs. Nye. We were hoping you could tell us that."

"Was it an accident?" She seemed very confused, as though she couldn't quite take it in. "Did he fall and hit his head?"

"It wasn't an accident," Witherspoon said gently. "Mr. Nye was murdered."

She gasped. "Murdered. You're not serious. You can't be. We're not the kind of people that get 'murdered'—" She broke off and her eyes filled with tears. "There must be some mistake. No one could murder Harrison." She turned away as sobs racked her body.

The housekeeper looked inquiringly at the inspector. He nodded, and she slipped her arm around her young mistress's shoulder. "There, there, Mrs. Nye."

"Why don't you take Mrs. Nye up to her room," Witherspoon instructed the housekeeper. It was obvious she was in no state to answer questions. "We'll have a word with the staff."

"Come on, my dear," the housekeeper said softly as she led the sobbing woman out of the room.

Barnes walked over to the bellpull and gave it a tug. The butler appeared a moment later. "You rang, sir?"

"I'm afraid we've some very bad news for the household," Witherspoon said. "Mr. Nye was found murdered early this morning."

The butler's mouth gaped open. "Murdered? Mr. Nye? But that's . . . that's . . . awful."

"Of course it is," the inspector agreed. He moved toward a settee. "Mrs. Nye took the news rather badly. She's resting in her room. Your housekeeper is taking care of her. But we'll need to question the staff. Can you arrange it please."

He hesitated again, his expression uncertain. "Well, I suppose it's all right."

The inspector understood the man's quandary. The master of the house was dead, and the mistress was hysterical, so there was no one to give them instructions. Witherspoon sat down on the settee. "Of course it's all right. I'm sure the staff wants to cooperate with the police. Now, why don't you go and arrange things. I'll take full responsibility for whatever happens."

Constable Barnes said. "Why don't I go with him and interview the kitchen staff?"

"Excellent idea." The inspector nodded approvingly, then looked at the butler. "Take the constable to your kitchen and then come back. I'll start with you."

Wiggins cautiously poked his head around the corner of Dunbarton Street and quickly stepped back out of sight. Blast a Spaniard! he thought. The whole street was crawling with police constables. He might have known. The inspector had probably ordered a house-to-house. Them ruddy constables would be there until they'd taken a statement from everyone who lived on the blooming street. That might take hours.

Sighing in disgust, he turned to go. "Ooh . . ." He was slammed from behind.

"Oh, I'm ever so sorry," a young woman carrying a wicker shopping basket said quickly. "I come flying around the corner so fast I wasn't looking where I was going. Are you all right?"

"I'm fine, miss. Really, it wasn't your fault. It was mine. I was dawdling." As she was a rather pretty girl with big brown eyes, dark hair tucked up under a plain white maid's cap and a lovely smile, he wanted to make a good impression on her.

"But I was walking too fast," she said quickly. "I must get to the shops." She gave him a cheeky grin and started to move past him.

But he'd been expecting that move and was ready for her. He fell into step beside her. "It were my fault. I was hangin' about because I'd 'eard there was a man found murdered 'ereabouts."

"He was killed right across the street from us. Mrs. Rather was all up in arms; just because her husband is day superintendent down at the pickle factory, she puts on airs. She didn't like havin' the police come 'round with all their questions, but that made no matter to them." She giggled. "It were ever such a sight watching her tryin' to be so high-and-mighty with that old police constable."

"The police asked you questions?" He made himself sound suitably impressed. He knew exactly how to handle her. Wiggins wasn't being arrogant, he simply knew how hard, boring and tedious it was working as a servant. Especially a lone maid in a small, working-class house like the ones on Dunbarton Street. It meant the girl did everything from scrubbing the floors to pounding the carpets and probably for very little pay as well. Anything that broke the monotony of the day-to-day drudgery, even murder, was to be welcomed. Everyone on Dunbarton Street would be talking about this killing for months.

Once they got over the shock of what had happened, they'd talk their heads off to anyone who'd stand still for ten seconds. "You mean you saw it 'appen? 'Ere, let me carry that basket for you. It looks 'eavy."

"Ta." She handed him her basket. "I'm only goin' up to the shops. Usually Mrs. Rather does all the shopping, but this here murder has got her all upset. Took to her bed, she did. My name's Kitty. Kitty Sparer."

"I'm Wiggins. Uh, if you're not in a 'urry, I'd be pleased to buy you a cup of tea and a bun at that café on Hurlingham Road. But you're probably in a rush . . ."

"I've a few minutes," she said. "Mrs. Rather was sound asleep when I left. To be honest, I was only rushin' up to the shops to see if anyone knew anything more about the murder. It's the most excitin' thing that's happened around here since Miss Geddy up and disappeared."

"I'm afraid I don't quite understand the question." The butler's heavy brows drew together in confusion.

Witherspoon didn't think it a particularly difficult question, but he knew the staff had had quite a shock and therefore probably weren't at their best. "What I want to know is if anything unusual happened to Mr. Nye last night?"

Duffy, the Nye butler, shrugged. "Not really, Mr. and Mrs. Nye hosted a dinner party last night, but that wasn't unusual. They had dinner parties every week or so."

"How many people were here?"

"The table was set for twelve, so there were ten guests."

"Can you get me a copy of the guest list?"

Duffy looked doubtful. "I don't think Mr. and Mrs. Nye's guests would appreciate the police pestering them with a lot of questions."

"Would you rather Mr. Nye's killer go free?"

"Or course not," he protested. "But . . . this is very difficult. Mrs. Nye is the great-niece of Lord Cavanaugh. She's very particular about observing the proper social

etiquette. With her indisposed, and Mr. Nye dead . . . oh
dear, I don't quite know what to do."

"I realize you're in a delicate situation, but murder is
murder. You really must cooperate. We need that guest
list. I'll take full responsibility." Witherspoon was amazed
that someone would be worried about etiquette when
there'd been murder done.

"I suppose it'll be all right." Duffy sighed and started
to get up.

The inspector waved him back to his seat. "You can
get it when we've finished. I've a few more questions. Do
you recall what time Mr. Nye left the house last night?"

"Oh dear, I'm not sure I know the exact time. But it
was quite late."

"Just give me your best estimate."

"I know it was after eleven." Duffy stroked his chin.
"Because I'd overheard Mrs. Ryker ask Mr. Ryker for the
time a few minutes before they actually left. They were
one of the last to leave, and I'd gotten them a hansom.
As I went back into the house to see if Mr. Lionel needed
a hansom as well, Mr. Nye was coming out. He didn't
say where he was going, he simply instructed me to leave
the back door unbolted."

"I see." Witherspoon nodded. "And you say this was
about eleven o'clock?"

Duffy thought for a moment. "Maybe fifteen past the
hour. I overheard the Rykers sometime before they actually left the house."

"You're sure Mr. Nye gave no indication of where he
was going?"

"None whatsoever, and it wasn't, of course, my place
to ask."

"Was Mr. Nye in the habit of going out late at night
by himself?" Witherspoon thought that a rather good
question.

"Well." Duffy frowned thoughtfully. "I wouldn't say
he was in the 'habit of doing' such a thing. But he was a
man who did as he pleased, if you get my meaning. There

were several other occasions I can think of when he went out late at night."

"Mrs. Nye didn't object?" the inspector asked. Being a lifelong bachelor, he was no expert on marriage, but he did think that wives tended to be curious about their husbands disappearing in the middle of the night.

The butler glanced over his shoulder to make sure no one was lurking about the hallway. Then he leaned closer to the inspector. "The first time it happened, she had a right fit. That was just after they married, two years ago."

"But he continued doing it?"

Again, the butler looked over his shoulder. "He kept on doing it, but after that terrible row, he never went out until after Mrs. Nye had retired for the night."

"Wasn't he concerned that she'd wake up and want to know where he was?" This was getting very curious.

"No. Mrs. Nye never gets up once she retires. As a matter of fact, from the day she came to this house as a bride, the staff had strict instructions not to bother her after she'd gone to bed. Seems the mistress is a very light sleeper, and once she gets awakened, she's up for hours. Of course, there are some in the household that think the mistress wasn't to be disturbed because . . . well . . . oh dear, I really oughtn't to say."

"Say what? I assure you anything you say will be held in the strictest confidence unless it directly involves Mr. Nye's murder," Witherspoon promised.

"Well, we think Mr. Nye didn't want us to disturb Mrs. Nye because she's tied to her bed. . . ."

The inspector felt a blush creep up his face.

"None of us have actually seen it," the butler continued quietly. "But it would certainly explain why the master and the mistress were insistent she never be disturbed. Of course it stands to reason, doesn't it?"

"Stands to reason," Witherspoon repeated. He was too embarrassed to even look at Barnes. He'd heard of people doing unusual things in the privacy of their own bedchambers, but it wasn't the sort of thing he was comfortable talking about.

"Of course it does," Duffy replied. "She could hurt herself otherwise. I'm sure it's rather undignified, but it's better than letting her get hurt when she begins her nocturnal rambling."

"Nocturnal rambling?" Barnes repeated. "Are you telling us that Mrs. Nye is tied to her bed because she sleepwalks?"

"That's what we think," Duffy said. "Not that we've discussed it very much, of course. Mr. Nye didn't allow us to gossip. But Mrs. Nye was seen walking about the garden in her nightclothes on at least two occasions. I guess she must have gotten loose on those nights."

Witherspoon sagged in relief. It sounded reasonable. People did walk in their sleep, and being tied to a bedpost could be rather undignified. He wouldn't want his servants seeing him in such a position. "Er, I take it she and her husband had separate bedrooms?"

"Of course. But there is, naturally, an adjoining door."

The inspector thought for a moment. He rather wanted to get off the subject of where people slept. "What did you mean when you said you came back inside to see if Mr. Lionel needed a cab?"

"Mr. Lionel was one of the dinner guests. He's a relation of Mrs. Nye, rather distant, I believe, but family nonetheless. He was actually the last to leave the house last night," Duffy explained. "After I passed Mr. Nye on the stairs I came back inside. Mr. Lionel and Mrs. Nye were in the drawing room. I asked Mr. Lionel if he needed a hansom. He said he didn't need one."

"Mr. Lionel lives close by?" Barnes asked.

"Not really, he has rooms in Bayswater. He generally has us fetch him a hansom, but last night he didn't. He said it was a nice evening, and he wanted to walk home."

"So Mrs. Nye hadn't retired by the time her husband left?" the inspector asked. "I thought you said he usually waited until she'd retired before he went out."

"He did," Duffy replied. "But last night he didn't, and I just assumed he must have told her something or other because she didn't seem upset. As a matter of fact, she smiled at him quite warmly before he left."

"So you think he probably told her where he was going?"

He hesitated. "I would think so. Mr. Nye is quite a strong character, if you know what I mean, but he's very considerate of his wife's feelings. He wouldn't want her to worry. I'm sure he must have mentioned something to Mrs. Nye. He was already a bit in the doghouse, if you know what I mean. What with that silly Mr. Daggett bursting in in the middle of the fish course and disrupting Mrs. Nye's dinner party."

Witherspoon stared hard at the man. "Would you mind explaining that please."

"Mr. Oscar Daggett, he's a business associate of Mr. Nye's. He showed up here last night in the middle of a dinner party and demanded to see the master. I tried to tell him that it was impossible, but he made such a fuss that Mr. Nye came out of the dining room to see what was going on. He took Mr. Daggett off to his study and they were in there for over half an hour. The mistress was most displeased."

"What time was this?"

"Let me see, we'd just served the trout . . ." His round face creased in concentration. "It must have been about half past eight. Yes, it was because the clock had just struck nine when Mrs. Nye left the table to go and get Mr. Nye."

"Where does this Mr. Daggett live?"

"I'm not sure of the exact address, but I believe his house is in South Kensington. His address is in Mr. Nye's study."

"Could you get it for me when you get the guest list?" Witherspoon asked. He tried to think of what would be best to ask next. There really were so very many questions one could ask when someone had been murdered. Sometimes it was difficult to decide which were the right ones. "Did Mr. Nye have any enemies?"

Duffy shook his head. "He was a decent enough master to the household. None of us would want to kill him."

"What about his business acquaintances?"

"I don't know anything about that."

"Has there been anyone lurking about the neighborhood or anything like that?"

"Not that I've noticed." Duffy smiled wearily. "I'm sorry. That's not much help."

"How long have you worked for Mr. Nye?"

"Since right before he and Mrs. Nye married two years ago." Duffy smiled sadly. "Let me explain, Inspector. Mr. Nye bought this house two years ago. Most of us were already here. We worked for Mr. Miselthorpe. When he passed away, Mr. Nye bought the house and hired us at the same time. We've all only worked for him for the past two years and in that time, it's been made quite clear to all of us that we'd best mind our own business."

"I see." The inspector nodded in understanding. "Are you saying that Mr. Nye was secretive?"

"I wouldn't exactly say that. But he did keep his business to himself. Not that it was ever necessary, of course. None of the staff would have ever dreamed of asking the master or mistress questions that didn't concern them." He paused. "This is difficult to explain, but Mr. Nye went out of his way to protect his privacy. The day he moved in he called the staff together and instructed us to mind our own affairs."

"Is that a common practice?" The inspector was rather sure it wasn't. In most large households, he'd noticed the servants didn't speak unless they'd been spoken to first.

"Of course not." Duffy pursed his lips. "We were all rather surprised. As a matter of fact, we weren't really sure what he was talking about. I could tell the rest of the staff was confused, so I asked Mr. Nye to clarify what he meant. He said if we were ever caught gossiping about him or his bride, that it would be grounds for instant dismissal."

The inspector said nothing for a moment as he digested this information. Then he asked, "Has anyone ever been dismissed for gossiping?" He was fairly certain the killer wasn't a disgruntled former servant. Harrison Nye didn't strike him as the type to go all the way to Fulham in the middle of the night to meet with a former maid or footman. But he felt he had to ask the question anyway.

"No one."

"Did you ever hear Mr. Nye mention someone called Miss Geddy?" The inspector held his breath, hoping against hope that there might be a connection between the victim and the place where he'd been found dead.

"No sir, I haven't. Is she a friend of Mr. Nye's?"

"We don't know. But he was found stabbed to death in her garden. Frankly, I was rather hoping you might have heard of her."

Betsy didn't want to be rude to Smythe, but honestly, if he didn't quit dogging her footsteps, she was going to scream. They'd separated when they reached Fulham, but every time she came out of a shop, there he was.

"Will you please go somewhere else," she said. She pointed toward the hansom stand at the end of Hurlingham Road. "There are cabs over there. Go talk to the drivers or something. Having you under my feet is making me nervous."

"I'm not tryin' to get under your feet," he insisted. "I'm trying to find that lad I was talking to this mornin'."

"Why don't you try looking on Dunbarton Street. Isn't that where he lives?" Betsy stepped off the curb, her destination a grocer's shop across the road.

"There's police all over Dunbarton Street." Smythe sighed and fell into step next to her. She shot him a glare. "Now, now, don't look so, lass. I'll not be interferin' on your patch. I'm takin' your advice and goin' up to the cabbie stand. Uh, 'ow much longer do you think you'll be?" The sun was sinking in the west, and he wanted to make sure they headed home together. She was an independent sort, but he didn't want her out on London's streets on her own once it got dark.

"The shops will be closing in another hour," she said. She knew he wouldn't give up, not this late in the day. She decided to give in gracefully. "I'll meet you at the omnibus stop over there"—she pointed back the way they'd come—"and we'll go home together. All right?"

"The omnibus will be crowded, we can take a hansom."

She opened her mouth to argue with him, then clamped it shut and grabbed his arm. "Oh no, don't look now, but there's Inspector Nivens."

Smythe looked in the direction she was staring. Nigel Nivens stood on the other side of the street, staring at the two of them. "Blast a Spaniard," he muttered. He quickly took Betsy's arm and waved at the inspector. " 'Ello, Inspector. Fancy seein' you 'ere."

Nivens waited till they'd reached the curb before he spoke. "I was just thinking the same about you two," he said. He stared at them suspiciously. "This is an awfully long way from Upper Edmonton Gardens, isn't it?"

"It's only a few miles," Smythe retorted. He racked his brain to think of a good reason for them being here.

"I wanted to see where the murder took place," Betsy said boldly. "It's my afternoon out, so I pestered Smythe into bringing me over here. Smythe and I are engaged, Inspector. Did you know that?"

Nivens's eyes widened a bit, but he managed to nod. "Congratulations."

Betsy could tell by the expression on his face that he got her point. He'd not pester her again; policeman or not, he was no match for Smythe in any way. "The inspector's cases are ever so interesting, don't you think so, Inspector Nivens?"

"I wouldn't exactly call murder 'interesting,' " Nivens said pompously.

"Inspector Witherspoon would." Smythe, who thought

he knew what Betsy was up to, decided to join in the fun. "Course, maybe that's why he's so good at catchin' killers. He thinks solvin' murders is real interestin' and real important too. Guess 'e just sees things in a different light as you."

Nivens flushed angrily. "That's not what I meant. Of course it's interesting, but it's hardly a spectator sport. I wouldn't go rushing over to visit the scene of a crime merely because I found it amusing."

"Are you on this case, then?" Betsy asked innocently. She knew he wasn't. "Is that why you're here? Mind you, I didn't realize you and our inspector would be working together again. I'll be sure and tell him we saw you this afternoon. . . ."

"We're not working together." Nivens's face turned even redder.

"Then you're like us, just 'ere to 'ave a bit of a snoop?" Smythe grinned amiably. He loved watching Nivens squirm.

"Certainly not," Nivens snorted. "I'm on my way to interview a robbery suspect over on Hobbs Lane. I do have cases of my own, you know. It's merely a coincidence that I ran into you two. I must be on my way." With a curt nod, he turned on his heel and hurried away.

Betsy sagged against Smythe in relief as they watched him disappear around the corner. "That was a close one."

"But you 'andled it just right. He'll not say a word to our inspector about seein' us 'ere."

Betsy giggled. "When I first spotted him, I started to panic a bit. Then I realized that sometimes you can get rid of a problem by just telling the truth. We are here because of the murder. Even if Nivens said something to our inspector about seeing us, it wouldn't make any difference. Inspector Witherspoon knows how curious we are about his cases."

"But it's not your day out," Smythe reminded her.

"The inspector isn't likely to know that, is he?" Betsy laughed. "He leaves that sort of thing to Mrs. Jeffries."

"That he does. Let's just hope that our inspector doesn't start to figure out that we do more than just have us a look at the murder scene. Speakin' of which, I'd best get to that hansom stand before they're all gone. It's gettin' late."

"And I want to have another go at that girl who works at the greengrocer's," Betsy said.

They each went their separate ways. Betsy was relieved that Smythe hadn't noticed the way she'd announced her engagement to Nivens. It might have led to some pointed questions, and she didn't want to have to lie to him. She retraced her steps and was soon back at the greengrocer's. But the young woman who'd been too busy to talk to her earlier was gone. Standing behind the counter was a tall, thin-faced young man wearing a dirty brown apron.

He glanced up as she entered the small enclosure. "Hello, miss, can I help you with something?" he asked.

Betsy gave him her best smile. "I'm not sure what I want," she said. "Those apples look very nice." She pointed to some pippins at the front of the large fruit bin. "I'll have three of them, please."

"Certainly, miss." He bustled out from behind the counter to get her order.

"Isn't it awful about that man being murdered?" she began. "Honestly, it makes a body frightened to go out the front door."

He shook his head in disbelief. "We were all shocked when we heard the news. Absolutely shocked. Things like that don't happen around here. This is a decent neighborhood. Not like some. Mind you, when I found out where the poor fellow was found, I wasn't surprised."

Betsy decided to play dumb. "Really? Why? What was so special about where he was found? I'll take one of those cauliflowers, too."

He put the apples on the counter. "You're not from around here, are you?"

"No," she admitted. She said nothing else and apparently that satisfied him because he kept on talking.

"He was found in Miss Geddy's front garden. She disappeared a couple of months back." He slapped a cauliflower down next to the apples. "Will there be anything else?"

Betsy wasn't about to lose him now. "Yes, I'll need some carrots. Have you got any pears?"

"We've some right over here." He went toward a bin on the other side of the apples.

"Do go on with what you were saying," she reminded him. "It was ever so interesting."

"I do hope this Mr. Daggett has something useful to tell us," Witherspoon said, as he and Barnes approached the front door of the town house on St. Albans Road in South Kensington. The sun had gone down behind the homes lining the west side of the road, plunging the area into the gray gloom of early evening.

"He must know something, sir," Barnes replied as he reached up and banged the door knocker. "According to what the footman told me, Daggett's visit was the reason Nye decided to go out last night. Otherwise, he'd have sent the footman to order him a hansom to pick him up at a prearranged time. The lad swears Nye always ordered a hansom in advance for his late-night outings. Besides, cabs are hard to find after ten o'clock."

The front door opened and a nervous-looking housemaid stuck her head out. "Oh, you're not Nelda."

"No, we're the police. Who's Nelda?" asked Witherspoon.

"She's the upstairs maid and she's been gone since last night," the maid said quickly. She glanced over her shoulder, took a deep breath and then plunged on. "Mrs. Benchley's all in a state about it and refuses to let us report her missing to the police. Mr. Daggett won't hear of it either, but I'm worried. I think we ought to do something."

"As we're here now, I think you'd better let us in," Barnes said calmly. The girl might chatter like a magpie, but he was fairly certain she'd spotted them coming, seen his uniform and beaten anyone else to the front door. Clever girl. The master of the house hadn't wanted the police called, but the lass had seen her chance and taken it.

"This way, please." She flung the door open wide and stepped back.

"Who is it, girl?" Oscar Daggett stepped out of the drawing room and into the hall just as the policemen stepped inside. "It's blasted inconvenient having Mrs. Benchley laid up like this. These girls don't know the proper way to open the door and announce people at all. . . ." He broke off complaining as he caught sight of the two men standing in his foyer.

"It's the police, sir," the girl said cheerfully. "They want to see you."

Witherspoon stepped forward. He was suddenly quite glad he'd listened to his constable instead of going home. This case was indeed getting strange. Another missing girl? What next? "I'm Inspector Gerald Witherspoon, and this is Constable Barnes," he said. "Are you Oscar Daggett?"

Daggett took a deep breath before he answered. "I am. What are you doing here? What do you want?"

"We'd like to speak to you, sir. We've a number of questions for you."

"If it's about that missing maid, it's all a tempest in a teapot." He glared at the maid. "I told you to leave the police out of this. How dare you go against my orders."

"I didn't go to the police," the girl protested. She edged behind the inspector. "Really I didn't, sir."

Witherspoon decided he didn't much care for Oscar Daggett. "We're here about an entirely different matter," he said firmly. "But if you've a missing girl in this household, we'd like to know about that as well."

"The girl isn't missing," he said, but he'd lost some of his bluster. "She's run off home. These country girls can't be trusted. Now, if you don't mind, I've an engagement for dinner, and I need to get dressed."

"We won't take much of your time," Barnes said. He gestured toward what he thought was probably the drawing room. "Can we sit down, please?" His words were polite enough, but the tone of his voice brooked no argument.

Daggett pursed his lips and turned on his heel. "This way," he muttered. He stalked toward an open doorway.

The maid scurried out from behind the inspector. "Nelda wouldn't have run off like that," she whispered. "She's a good girl, and she's my friend. She'd have told me if she was going home, besides, she wouldn't leave her young man. I don't care what he says. Something's happened to her."

"Don't worry, we'll be down to speak to you about your missing friend," Witherspoon assured the girl, as he and Barnes followed Daggett.

"Thank you, sir." She hurried off down the hall.

They entered a nicely furnished drawing room. It was done in masculine colors of forest green and brown. There were the usual hunting scenes on the wall and heavy, dark-upholstered furniture. Daggett sat on a chair near the marble fireplace. "What's this about?" He didn't invite them to sit down.

Witherspoon didn't mind standing up. As a matter of fact, sometimes he thought being on his feet gave him a distinct advantage. "Do you know a man named Harrison Nye?"

Daggett nodded slowly. "Yes. I've known him for over fifteen years. We were in business together."

"What kind of business, sir?" Barnes asked.

"A variety of things, Inspector. Insurance, shipping, mining, overseas investments." He waved his arm expansively. "As I said, a number of things. Now, what's this all about?"

"When was the last time you spoke with Mr. Nye?" Witherspoon asked.

"Last night. I popped around to have a word with him about a business matter." He shrugged. "Unfortunately, he was in the middle of a dinner party. But we had a quick word together. Why?"

"Harrison Nye was murdered last night." Witherspoon watched Daggett carefully.

Daggett's mouth dropped open. He bolted up from his chair. "Murdered! But that's absurd. No one would murder Harrison."

"But I'm afraid someone did," the inspector said. "Do you happen to know if Mr. Nye had any enemies?"

"He was a businessman. He could be ruthless at times, but I don't know of anyone who'd actually want to murder him."

CHAPTER 4

By the time Inspector Witherspoon climbed the stairs to his front door, his head was pounding and there was a dull ache in his lower back.

Mrs. Jeffries was waiting for him in the front hall. "Good evening, sir," she said cheerfully.

"Good evening, Mrs. Jeffries." He handed her his bowler hat. "I'm sorry to be so late. I do hope Mrs. Goodge isn't put out."

"Not at all, sir. We're all quite used to your odd hours. She's kept your supper warm, sir. I'll just nip down and bring it up."

"Oh, do let's have a sherry first," Witherspoon suggested. "It's been a long day."

"Of course, sir." Mrs. Jeffries hid a smile as she led the way down the hall. This was even better than she'd hoped. He was always so much more willing to talk about his cases over a glass of sherry.

The inspector followed her into the drawing room. He plopped down in his favorite chair as she poured them both a glass of Harvey's. "Here you are, sir." She gave him a sympathetic smile. "You do look a bit tired. Have you had a very difficult time? Betsy mentioned you'd been sent out on a murder."

"Actually"—he took a sip from his glass—"I'm quite pleased with the progress we've made so far. One never likes to think that murder is by any means commonplace"—he sighed—"but there does seem to be a lot of it about these days."

"I suspect there always has been, sir," she replied honestly. "Perhaps in earlier times it was simply easier to hide it than it is now. If you ask me, sir, that's a step in the right direction."

"How right you are, Mrs. Jeffries." He sighed. "Of course, it isn't always easy to distinguish between a natural death and a deliberate murder. I imagine that before the formation of the police, people were popping one another off all the time. There's a number of poisons that simulate heart failure or seizure." He shook his head in dismay.

"Is that how your victim in today's murder died?" she asked innocently.

"Not quite. Poor fellow was stabbed. It was obviously murder."

"How awful, sir." She clucked her tongue. "You've had a lot of stabbings in the last couple of years."

"Only because it's easier for people to get hold of knives than it is guns or poison," he replied with a sad smile. "But nevertheless, I do believe I've already got a suspect for this one."

Mrs. Jeffries didn't like the sound of that. It could only mean one thing, if after less than one day on the case, the inspector already thought he knew who did it, then there probably wasn't much of a mystery to solve. Drat. "So soon? How very clever of you, sir."

"Well, I don't want to get too far ahead of myself, but we do have someone we're keeping our eye on. His story doesn't really ring true, if you know what I mean."

"I'm afraid I don't, sir," she said. "You haven't really told me anything about your case at all."

He took another swig of sherry. "I am getting ahead of myself. Do forgive me, I know how very interested you are in my work. The victim was a man named Harrison Nye. Quite a wealthy fellow, judging by the house he owns. But then again, appearances can be deceiving. For all I know the house may be mortgaged to the hilt and there might have been creditors hounding the fellow every day." He continued talking for the next half hour, filling the housekeeper in on all the details he'd gleaned thus far.

Mrs. Jeffries listened carefully, tucking everything she heard safely into her phenomenal memory.

"So you can understand why I want to keep my eye on Oscar Daggett," he finished. "There was something odd about the man's behavior. Mind you, we've got to pop back in the morning. It's imperative we have a word with Daggett's staff."

"I take it you don't believe he was home when he claimed to be," Mrs. Jeffries asked. Her mind was working furiously. Coupled with the information she already had from the others, she knew this case was more complex than the inspector thought. There were already far too many questions that needed answers.

"It's not that so much as it is what one of the maids told us when we first arrived. It seems a girl has disappeared from the place. A maid called Nelda Smith. I feel a bit bad, actually, I told one of the other young women in the household I'd come down to the kitchen and talk to her about her missing friend before I left. But Daggett was insistent we leave as he had a dinner engagement. Not to worry, though, I've got a constable watching the house. The girl should be all right until tomorrow." He put his glass down and got to his feet. "Not that I think she's in any danger, of course. But short of arresting the fellow, I couldn't do anything else but leave when he made such a fuss."

"I'm sure you did right, sir."

"Thank you, one does worry in these sorts of cases. I would hate for the girl to think I was ignoring her."

"What was the girl's name?" Mrs. Jeffries asked.

"What girl?"

"The one who wanted to talk with you about the missing girl?"

"Hortense Rivers. She seemed quite concerned. But Daggett insisted the missing maid had gone back home to the country." He sighed and put down his glass. "I believe I'll have my tray now if you don't mind, Mrs. Jeffries."

"Of course, sir." She had dozens of questions she intended to ask. "If you'll go into the dining room, I'll pop down and get your supper."

The next morning, Mrs. Jeffries rushed down to the kitchen the moment she closed the door behind Inspector Witherspoon. The others were waiting for her when she entered the kitchen. Even Luty and Hatchet were sitting in their usual spots at the kitchen table.

"The inspector's finally gone, has he?" Mrs. Goodge looked up over the rim of her spectacles. "It took him long enough."

"I thought he was gonna camp out in the dining room all mornin'," Luty declared, "and we've got lots to talk about."

"He's gone." Mrs. Jeffries slipped into her chair at the head of the table. "Should I tell you everything I learned from the inspector last night, or would you all like to have your say first?"

"I'd like to have my say first, please," Betsy said. "I don't know why, it just seems to make more sense when we do our bit first."

"I agree," Mrs. Goodge said stoutly. "Even though I haven't got much to report. As a matter of fact, I've got nothing to report. But I've got a number of sources coming through the kitchen today, so by tomorrow I'll be able to hold up my end of the stick."

The housekeeper nodded at Betsy. "Go ahead, tell us what you've learned."

"Well, it doesn't amount to much, but I did hear a bit about the woman who disappeared. The one who owns the house where the murder took place."

"You mean that Miss Geddy person?" Wiggins clarified.

"Of course she means Miss Geddy." The cook frowned at the lad. "Who else has disappeared and had a murder on their front steps?"

"I like to keep me facts straight." Wiggins sniffed. "It's not good to get muddled, especially at the beginning of an investigation."

"How very prudent of you, Wiggins," Mrs. Jeffries said soothingly. "Do go on, Betsy."

"According to the gossip I got, this Miss Geddy kept very much to herself. But the local shopkeepers liked her all right, she paid her bills on time and didn't ask for credit."

"How'd she pay?" Smythe asked.

Betsy looked surprised by the question. "I don't know, I never thought to ask. Is it important?"

"Probably not." He shrugged. "But it never hurts to know these things. Go on, lass, I didn't mean to interrupt."

"Well, like I was saying, the shopkeepers like her well enough, but she wasn't very popular about the neighborhood."

"How unpopular was the lady?" Hatchet asked.

"She had a tart tongue if she was crossed. She had a run-in at the local post office," Betsy said. "She used to go in there to mail off packages, and the poor man behind the counter made some comment about it. You know, he was trying to be friendly like, make conversation, that sort of thing. But Miss Geddy flew right off the handle. Told the man it was his job to mail the parcel, not make comments for all and sundry to hear her personal business. The post office was full when this happened. There were dozens of people lined up. They all heard it. It caused quite a stir in the neighborhood. More importantly, it happened just a few days before she disappeared."

"How very interesting," Mrs. Jeffries commented. "Anything else?"

"That's about it, I'm afraid." Betsy sighed. "I wish I could have found out where this Miss Geddy was mailing off her parcels to, but no one I spoke to knew that. Do you think it's important?"

Mrs. Jeffries had no idea what was important or what wasn't important. "Find out if you can," she replied. "At this point in the investigation, we don't know what is or isn't important. Who would like to go next?"

"I've not got anything to report," Smythe said. "None of the drivers I talked to had taken any fares to Dunbarton Street. I thought I'd make the rounds of the pubs today and see if I can pick up anythin' there."

"That's an excellent idea." Mrs. Jeffries nodded encouragingly.

"Can I go now?" Wiggins asked. At the housekeeper's nod, he continued. "I met up with a maid that lives across the street from the killin'. Her name's Kitty Sparer. I didn't learn all that much. She was a right talker, but she didn't know much of anything. Nice girl, though."

"Did you find out anything at all?" Mrs. Goodge asked. "Or was your whole afternoon a complete waste of time?"

"I wouldn't call it a complete waste," Wiggins replied cheerfully. "She did tell me that she heard footsteps going up Miss Geddy's walkway last night."

"She heard the killer?" Luty said eagerly.

Wiggins's face fell. "I don't think so. She heard the footsteps fairly early in the evening. She didn't know the time, just that it was early like in the evenin', so it couldn't 'ave been the killer." He shrugged.

"Did she see anyone or just hear footsteps?" Mrs. Jeffries asked.

"She only heard the footsteps," Wiggins replied. "She

was busy with the mistress of the house so she couldn't get to the window to 'ave a look."

"How did she know where they were?" Luty snorted. "Seems to me if she only heard footsteps, then how could she tell they was goin' up this Miss Geddy's walkway?"

"She knew it was Miss Geddy's walkway because the steps were shoes on stone, not shoes on dirt. The footpath along Dunbarton Street isn't paved. Miss Geddy's walkway is done in stone. It's the only one along there that is. The road's made of brick, and there's a streetlamp down the far end, but the local council's never paved the footpath. The residents have complained about it, but it's not done any good."

"Wasn't she curious that she heard footsteps on the walkway of an empty house?" Hatchet asked.

"Course she was," he said. "But her mistress was jawin' at 'er something fierce, and by the time she could get away and have a look out the front window, there was nothing there."

"That's very interesting," Mrs. Jeffries muttered. "I do hope she'll have a word with the police and let them know what she heard."

"She will," Wiggins said cheerfully. "She thinks this murder is the most excitin' thing that's ever 'appened. That's all I've got to report."

"Can I go next?" Luty asked. "I found out that Harrison Nye has a list of enemies as long as my right arm, and I'm dying to tell everyone."

"Really, madam." Hatchet sniffed disapprovingly. "You mustn't exaggerate so. You told me yourself it was only his banker and solicitor that disliked him."

"That's a list." Luty sniffed. "Besides, it wasn't just one solicitor, it was two. They were brothers, and they blame Nye for ruining their business."

"Gracious, Luty, that certainly sounds like motive for murder."

"That's what I thought too," Luty said.

"What happened?" Betsy asked eagerly.

"Nye blamed his solictors for making so many errors on a piece of property he was tryin' to buy that it cost him the deal. They made a bunch of mistakes, and by the time it was sorted out, the man who owned the property had died and his heirs then refused to sell. The whole business cost Nye a lot of money. He'd already raised a packet of cash from a group of private investors, and he ended up givin' it all back."

"And Nye blamed his lawyers?" Smythe raised his eyebrows. "But Nye's the one who's dead, not them."

"Yeah, but he sued the solicitors for damages and actually won. Cost 'em so much they went bankrupt." She grinned at the surprised expression on the faces around the table. "I know, I found it hard to believe too. Usually the legal profession protects its own. But from what I heard, these two were more incompetent than most. Anyway, they had reason to hate Harrison Nye's guts."

"Did you get their names?" Betsy asked.

"It's Windemere," she replied. "John and Peter Windemere."

Mrs. Jeffries tapped her fingers against her heavy, brown mug. This was quite interesting. It was rare that one heard of solicitors actually being sued by their clients, rarer still that the clients actually won. "When did this happen?"

"It's been a couple of years back." Luty hedged.

"A couple of years," Hatchet exclaimed. He snorted derisively. "Really, madam, it happened eleven years ago."

"So what? Sometimes people let their anger fester forever before it boils up and causes them to go dotty. That could have been what happened here. They coulda bided their time until they caught him alone late one night and then did their worst . . ."

"So you're saying they hung around his home waiting for the one time he went out at night unexpectedly, followed him and then murdered him in the front garden of a strange house in Fulham?" Hatchet's voice dripped sarcasm.

"I didn't say it did happen that way, I said it mighta happened that way." She glared at her butler. "Besides, at least I come up with something. You ain't doin' so good, are ya?"

He glared right back at her. "I won't dignify that remark with a response. Investigating a murder doesn't require speed, madam, it requires perseverance."

"Which you both have in abundance," Mrs. Jeffries interjected. She rather agreed with Hatchet; it was highly unlikely the disgraced solicitors had waited eleven years to take their revenge, but it wasn't impossible either. Furthermore, she knew something they didn't. She had a copy of the guest list in her pocket. "Luty, could you find out a bit more about the Windemere brothers? You know, find out their financial circumstances, that sort of thing."

Luty smiled smugly. "I intended to do just that. Plus, I've got my sources workin' on findin' out more about our victim."

"Why'd 'is banker dislike 'im?" Wiggins asked.

Luty waved her hand dismissively. "For the same reason the solicitors did, he tried to ruin the fellow in a dispute over a letter of credit. Only Marcus Koonts was smarter than them solictors and hired a decent barrister. Nye lost the case but not before he'd caused Koonts a lot of trouble. Besides, Marcus couldn't have killed Nye. He's been in Scotland since last week. He might hate Nye, but he's no killer. I've known him for years."

"I still wish I could remember where I'd 'eard that name," Smythe said. He shook his head. Perhaps he'd make a run down to the docks and have a chat with one of his sources, Blimpey Groggins.

"Does anyone else have anything to report?" Mrs. Jeffries glanced around the table. "Well, then, I'll tell you what I learned from the inspector." She poured herself another cup of tea as she spoke. This might take a while, and she didn't want to leave out anything. They were going to have a lot to do today, and she wanted everyone to be prepared with as much knowledge as possible.

The inspector didn't particularly care for graveyards. He felt they were a tad depressing. But as Mr. Moff had already gone to work by the time he and Constable Barnes had arrived at the Moff home, he had no choice but to go along to the Fulham Cemetery. The entrance was off the Fulham Palace Road. Witherspoon stopped and stared across the open fields of the common. The grass was still green, but the trees had lost most of their leaves, and the air was crisp enough that he was glad he wore his good black greatcoat. In the distance, the mist rose from the river, and the weak autumn sun would make no headway in burning through the thick cloud layer above. All in all it was a depressing gray day, and he was stuck interviewing a witness at a cemetery. Drat.

"Shall we go in, sir?" Barnes inquired. He tried not to smile at the glum expression on the inspector's face. "It won't be too bad, sir."

"Yes, I suppose we must." Witherspoon started through the open iron gates. He stopped just inside and peered through the rows of crowded headstones and gated crypts. "I wonder where the porters' lodge or the caretaker's place might be."

"Are you lookin' for me, then," a voice said from behind them.

Witherspoon jumped and whirled about. Even Barnes was a bit startled. A tall, thin man dressed in a gray shirt and dark gray trousers stood just inside the gate. He held a shovel in his right hand. His eyes were as gray as his clothes and his face was long and weather-beaten. "Are you Mr. Moff?"

"The missus said you'd be wanting to have a word with me," he replied. "You'll have to talk to me while I work, we've one comin' in this morning at ten and that stupid lad's not got the hole dug deep enough." He turned and began weaving his way through a row of headstones.

Witherspoon glanced at Barnes, shrugged and trailed after their witness. They followed him to the north corner of the cemetery, then the fellow seemed to disappear. "I say." Witherspoon came to a halt on the far side of an open pit. "Where'd the man go?"

"I'm right here." This time the voice came from below them. "I expect you're wantin' to ask me if I know anything about that fellow that got himself killed on Miss Geddy's walkway."

Witherspoon looked down and realized Mr. Moff was standing in an open grave. He leapt to one side as a shovelful of dirt came flying out and landed inches away from his good black shoes.

"Did you hear anything unusual?" Barnes asked. He'd moved to the other side of the grave and whipped out his little brown notebook.

"Nah, once I'm in bed, I'm dead to the world." He looked up and grinned. "If you'll pardon the expression."

The inspector didn't think that was particularly funny. Gracious, didn't the fellow have any respect for the dead? "What time did you retire that night?" He thought it was a fairly useless question, but he had to start somewhere.

"Right after nine." Moff went back to his digging. "The missus and I had a bit of a natter and then I went out to the pub for a quick one. I was back by a quarter to, had a wash and then went to bed. The missus was already asleep."

"Did you happen to see anyone hanging about the neighborhood while you were coming back from the pub?" Witherspoon pulled his handkerchief out and whipped a bit of dirt off his sleeve.

Moff stopped and rested on the end of his shovel. "Well, I did see that young girl in Miss Geddy's front garden, but I wouldn't say she was hanging about. She was at the front door."

"You mean she was knocking?" Barnes asked.

"I didn't see her knockin'." He went back to his digging. "I told her that no one lived there, and that seemed to upset her some."

"Upset her how?" Witherspoon leaned closer. This was finally getting interesting.

"She didn't start blubberin' or anything like that," Moff replied. "She said something like 'oh bother,' or 'I'll not bother then,' I'm not sure. I weren't payin' all that much attention to the girl. I was in a hurry to get home."

"You didn't think it strange that she was at the door of an empty house?" Barnes asked. "It's our understanding that Miss Geddy, the owner, disappeared some months ago."

"That's true." Moff looked up at the constable and shrugged. "She up and bolted one night."

"Bolted? That's an unusual choice of words," Witherspoon said.

He shrugged. "What else would you call it when someone sneaks out in the middle of the night?"

"You saw her leave?" Witherspoon asked eagerly. Gracious, this case was getting complicated. He'd no idea how Miss Geddy's disappearance related to Harrison Nye's murder, but he knew it did. He could feel it in his bones.

"I did. Had a bit of indigestion that night, so I got up to get one of the missus's bilious pills. She swears by Cockles, she does, and it did help a bit. When I went back to bed, I happened to glance out the window, and I saw her leavin'. Our bedroom overlooks the street."

"Did she have any baggage?" Barnes asked.

He frowned for a moment, then brightened as the memory returned. "She had a carpetbag with her. I remember because she kept banging it on the side of the hansom when she was climbin' inside."

"Miss Geddy left in a hansom," Witherspoon clarified. He wanted to make sure he understood.

"That's what I said." Moff went back to his task.

"If you don't mind my sayin' so, sir," Barnes said, "the whole neighborhood keeps talking about how this woman disappeared, and you said nothing to anyone, including your own wife, about Miss Geddy leaving of her own free will."

"I know." Moff grinned widely. "It's been a right old laugh watchin' all them tongues waggin'. You should hear some of the things they've been sayin'." He cackled. "I haven't had so much fun in years. Some claim she's been sold to white slavers, some claim that bloke she had a run-in with down at the post office come after her and did her in, and the rest say she were runnin' off to meet her lover. I tell ya, it's been a right old bust-up." He laughed again and went back to shoveling dirt.

Barnes and Witherspoon looked at one another. The constable sighed. "Do you have any idea where Miss Geddy went?" he asked.

"The train station," Moff replied. "I heard her tell the driver to take her to Victoria Station. It was almost midnight and quiet enough to hear a pin drop. I'm surprised I'm the only one who heard her. She weren't botherin' to be quiet about it, and the hansom made enough noise to wake the dead."

"Do you happen to recall exactly what the date was?" Witherspoon asked. He didn't hold out much hope the man would remember. It was, after all, two months ago.

"Course I do," he said proudly. "It was August 12."

The inspector raised his eyebrows. "Gracious, you do have a remarkable memory."

"Not really," Moff admitted. "The only reason I remember is because of my indigestion. I always get it when we go to Winnie's for supper. She's my sister-in-law. It was her husband's fiftieth birthday, and we was havin' a bit of celebration. She's a good enough woman, our Winnie, nice disposition and all that. But she's a terrible cook. Her Yorkshire puddin' was sittin' on my stomach somethin' awful. Kept me awake for hours, it did."

Witherspoon nodded sympathetically. He wished Mr. Moff had gone to Winnie's for supper the night before last; if he had, he might have seen the murder. "Have you ever heard of a man called Harrison Nye?"

"That's the bloke that was murdered," Moff said. "Never heard of him."

"You seem an observant sort of fellow," Barnes said quickly. "I don't suppose you remember someone fitting Nye's description ever coming around to visit Miss Geddy?"

Witherspoon smiled approvingly at the constable. That was a jolly good question.

Moff shook his head. "Nah, she never had any visitors. Mind you, she used to go to the post office quite a bit. She was always mailin' off packages."

"You mentioned she had a 'bit of a run-in with some bloke at the post office'?" Witherspoon didn't think Miss Geddy's disappearance or Harrison Nye's murder had anything to do with an angry postal worker. Civil servants didn't generally come after every member of the public whom they'd had words with, but one never knew.

"You'll need to ask my wife about that set-to," Moff said. He stopped and wiped the sweat off his brow. "She knows all about it. I only heard it secondhand-like. Is there anything else?"

The inspector couldn't think of anything. He looked hopefully at Barnes, but he closed his notebook and slipped it into the pocket of his uniform. "No, sir, there's nothing else. But do contact me if you think of anything else that may be helpful in our inquiries."

Moff grunted agreeably but didn't look up.

Wiggins started to reach for another sticky bun. "So what do we do now?"

Mrs. Goodge pushed the plate out of his reach. "Don't be so greedy. If you eat another, you'll make yourself sick."

"I've only 'ad two," he protested, but he pulled his hand back.

"And you've had upset stomach three times this month," the cook said tartly.

"But you do have a point," the housekeeper interjected smoothly. "What do we do now? We've learned an enormous amount of information, but I'm in a bit of a muddle as to where we ought to focus our attention." They now were in the position of having almost too many avenues of inquiry to pursue.

"I think we ought to do what we always do," Betsy said, "and concentrate on the victim."

"But what about this Daggett fellow?" Smythe argued. "Seems to me it was his visit to Nye that got the fellow killed."

"We don't know that for certain," she replied.

"The bloke barged into a dinner party and insisted on seein' Nye. A few hours later, he was dead."

"But we don't know that Daggett's visit was the reason Nye went to Fulham that night. He may have been planning on going out all along. The inspector told Mrs. Jeffries that Nye had a habit of going out on his own at night."

"But he always waited until his wife had retired for the night," Smythe reminded them. "But this time, he didn't even wait until all his dinner guests had gone before he left. And from what the inspector told Mrs. Jeffries, Constable Barnes found out from the Daggetts' servants that he got up from his sickbed to go to Nye's so whatever sent him there, it must have been important."

"I think you're both right," Mrs. Jeffries said quickly. She meant it too. She had a feeling this case was going to be very, very complex. It was imperative they obtain as much information as possible, especially at this stage of the investigation. "The victim, of course, is important, but so is Oscar Daggett." She cocked her head to one side and gazed appraisingly around the table. "There are enough of us to do both. We'll have to scatter our resources a bit thinly, but I don't think that's going to be a problem."

Hatchet leaned forward, his expression thoughtful. "Precisely what does that mean? In practical terms, that is."

"It means some of us need to concentrate on learning everything we can about Harrison Nye and the rest of us need to concentrate on Daggett."

"I'll take Nye," Smythe volunteered. "It's nigglin' me that I can't remember where I've heard of him."

"I'll get my sources workin' on both of them," Mrs. Goodge said. "And Mrs. Nye too. Didn't you say she's some relation to Lord Cavanaugh? I only wish we had the names of the guests at the dinner party."

"We do," Mrs. Jeffries said. "The inspector had the dinner guest list in his coat pocket. I slipped down here last night and copied the names out."

"You went through the inspector's pockets!" Wiggins was positively scandalized.

"Of course she went through his pockets," Luty exclaimed. "This is murder we're investigatin'. Sometimes you have to ignore the social niceties. We need all the clues we can git. Don't be such a Goody Two-shoes, boy. It ain't like the man keeps love letters or personal stuff in his pockets."

"Thank you, Luty," Mrs. Jeffries said gratefully. Then she looked at the footman. "I don't want you to think I'm in the habit of violating the inspector's privacy. I only searched the pockets of his overcoat and only then if he's mentioned that he got a list of some sort or another."

"I weren't tryin' to make out like you was doin' something wrong." Wiggins blushed a deep red. He knew the housekeeper wouldn't do anything really wrong. "I was just a bit surprised, that's all."

"Mrs. Jeffries knows that," Smythe said. He could tell that the footman was genuinely embarrassed. "I think you ought to have a gander 'round the Daggett household. You're always right good at gettin' the servants to talk, especially housemaids and such."

"Ya think so?" Wiggins brightened immediately.

"We all think it," Betsy interjected. She gave Smythe a fast, grateful smile. He might be big and hard-looking, but he was the best man in the world. Beneath that rough exterior, he truly had a heart of gold. She loved him more than her own life, and she was pleased to be marrying him; she only hoped he wouldn't pressure her to do it too quickly. But she felt fairly certain he wouldn't push her too hard. He loved their investigations too. "And if you've a mind to head over Daggett's way this afternoon, I'll go along with you. I want to have a word with the local shopkeepers in the area."

"I suppose I'd best keep on seein' what I can suss out about Nye," Luty said. "Iffen that's all right with everyone. I can put out a few feelers about Oscar Daggett as well."

"And let's not forget the missing woman," Hatchet reminded them. "Apparently, it seems this Miss Frieda Geddy's disappearance may have some bearing on the case."

"Would you like to follow up that inquiry?" Mrs. Jeffries asked. It would be easier to keep everything straight if they were somewhat organized in their investigation.

"Certainly, though I do wish we knew precisely when she disappeared. But never fear, I'm sure with my rather extensive network of information sources, I'll soon find out everything we need to know."

"Don't be so modest, Hatchet." Luty laughed.

"Modesty has nothing to do with it, madam. I'm merely stating a fact." He smiled cheerfully. "I have great confidence in all of us."

Luty snorted. "You have more in yourself, though."

"Nonsense, we've all had tremendous successes in our endeavors. What is this, our fifteenth case?" He was toying with the notion of writing a comprehensive history of everything they'd done thus far, but he'd not made up his mind yet. It would involve rather a lot of work.

"Our sixteenth, your fifteenth and Mrs. Jeffries's seventeenth," Wiggins stated matter-of-factly.

Everyone gaped at him.

He shrugged. "I've been keepin' track."

"I can see where Hepzibah"—Luty jerked her chin at the housekeeper—"has one more than me and Hatchet. After all, she started this whole thing by figurin' out them horrible Kensington High Street murders, but I can't see where you all"—she jerked her head in a circle, indicating the rest of them—"have any more cases than us."

"But we do," Wiggins explained. "We helped solve that Dr. Slocum's murder."

"And I think we ought to count the horrible Kensington High Street murders as well," Mrs. Goodge added. "We helped with that one."

"But we didn't know we was helpin'," Wiggins pointed out, "so it don't count."

"It does too," Betsy said flatly. "We helped, and that's that. Besides, we each figured it out on our own before the case actually got solved."

"But Mrs. Jeffries didn't tell us what she was up to until after Dr. Slocum had been poisoned," Wiggins insisted. "So we can't count it as one of ours."

"That's daft," Mrs. Goodge yelped.

"Of course we can count it," Smythe said.

"I think I ought to count the Slocum murder," Luty argued, "I give you plenty of information that helped solve the case, and I figured out what all of you was up to."

"If you get to count that one, then so do I," Hatchet interjected. "I was the one that spotted Miss Betsy and Wiggins asking questions about the neighborhood. You'd have never figured out it was the inspector's household solving the murder if I hadn't told you."

"You only spotted 'em," Luty yelped in outrage. "It was me that figured out what they was up to."

Hatchet's eyebrows rose halfway up to his hairline. "Really, madam, are you having trouble with your memory . . . ?"

"You can all count all of them," Mrs. Jeffries interrupted. She gazed sternly around the table. "Honestly, I don't know why it's so important to you, but the truth is, all of you have helped on all the cases. Except of course, for Luty and Hatchet on the Kensington High Street murders. Now, can we get on with it? We've not got all day, and we do have a killer to catch." But the argument rattled her so much she forgot to mention that both of the Windemere brothers were at the top of the guest list.

CHAPTER 5

Inspector Witherspoon stood in the tiny servants' hall of Oscar Daggett's home. "I say, Constable, for such an apparently wealthy man, he certainly doesn't bother to make his staff comfortable."

The room was pathetically furnished, the long oak table was scratched and stained, the chairs were mismatched and rickety, the floor was plain wood without so much as a scrap of carpet, and the small cabinet that probably held the sugar and tea was padlocked shut.

"He takes good care of himself but can't even spare a tablecloth for his staff," Barnes muttered in disgust.

"Unfortunately, most of the servants' halls in London are at this sort of standard. I don't know why." He shook his head in disbelief. "You'd think people who had so much could spare a few bob a year to make their servants' lives a bit easier. But they never do, do they?"

"You do, sir," Barnes said. "Your servants eat as well as you, sleep in comfortable beds and spend their relaxing hour in that nice big kitchen of yours. So you can't say that everyone treats their staff badly."

"Do you have any positions open?" a timid voice asked from behind them.

They turned and saw Hortense, the maid, standing in the doorway. "I'm sorry, I wasn't tryin' to eavesdrop. But I couldn't help overhearin' and frankly, sir, you sound like a good man to work for." She snorted. "Course just about anywhere'd be better than here."

"Oh dear," Witherspoon replied. "I don't have any positions open right at this moment, but I will keep you in mind if I need anyone. I'm sorry I wasn't able to have a word with you yesterday, but Mr. Daggett insisted we leave."

Barnes covered his mouth with his hand in an effort to turn his laughter into a cough. His inspector was brilliant at solving murders, but the poor man was as innocent as a kitten when it came to dealing with people. Especially female people.

"That's all right, sir." Hortense marched into the room. "I overheard him telling you to go. Scared me a bit, it did. I thought for certain I was in for the sharp side of his tongue after you'd gone, but he never said a word. He just shut himself up in his study until it was time for bed."

"I'm glad you didn't suffer for telling us about the girl that's gone missing," Witherspoon said. He was greatly relieved that nothing untoward had happened to the girl. "Why don't we sit down, Hortense, and we can have a nice chat about your friend."

"I was afraid you weren't goin' to come back," Hortense said as she scurried over to the table and flopped down in one of the chairs. "I kept tellin' Mrs. Benchley that we had to tell someone about Nelda. Her things is still here, ya know. She wouldn't have run home without her trunk. I don't care what Mr. Daggett says. Somethin' has happened to her."

Witherspoon took a seat next to the girl, and Barnes eased his tall frame into the chair at the end. He whipped out his notebook. "Why don't you tell us what happened, lass," he said softly, "and the best way for us to really understand is for you to start at the beginning."

"All right, I guess that's best, I do tend to get muddled when I'm excited." Hortense took a long, deep breath. "It all started day before yesterday. Mr. Daggett took one of his sick spells, and we had to send off for Dr. Wiltshire."

"Dr. Wiltshire?" Witherspoon clarified. "Is his surgery close by?"

"It's just around the corner on Victoria Road. Which is lucky for us," Hortense charged. "Otherwise, we'd run our feet off. Mr. Daggett's always sending us for the doctor."

"I take it his health isn't very good," Witherspoon asked.

"He's as healthy as a ruddy workhorse," Hortense exclaimed. "But he's got more aches and pains than a dog has fleas. Even the doctor gets fed up with him."

Barnes looked up from his notebook. "What happened after you got the doctor around?"

"Doctor couldn't come right away. He told me to tell Mr. Daggett to go to bed and he'd be along as soon as he could get away." Hortense pursed her lips. "Course when I told Mr. Daggett it'd be a while before Dr. Wiltshire come to see him, he got so angry I thought he'd pop. But he didn't. He took to his bed and had all of us, but especially Nelda, fetchin' and carryin' and runnin' up and down those ruddy back stairs for hours. Finally, when the doctor got here, all Mr. Daggett had wrong with him was a bit of indigestion."

Witherspoon frowned thoughtfully. "So Mr. Daggett was ill enough that he stayed in bed, is that what you're saying?"

She nodded eagerly. "Right, took to his bed from the first pain, had poor Nelda runnin' up with fresh nightshirts every hour, he did, and he made her change the bed."

"So when did Nelda leave?" Barnes asked.

"Oh, I'm not sure I know what time it was exactly." Hortense wrinkled her forehead. "Things were in a bit of a mess, you see, what with Mrs. Benchley bleedin' all over the kitchen and us having to send for Dr. Wiltshire again. . . ." She paused. "That's right, it was right after Mrs. Benchley had the accident that Nelda left. She took a letter that Mr. Daggett had given her, and she ain't been seen since."

Barnes and Witherspoon glanced at each other. Daggett hadn't mentioned giving the girl an errand. "What's Nelda's last name?" the inspector asked.

"Smith," she replied promptly. "Nelda Smith. She's from a small village in Lancashire. She's only been in London for a couple of months. She didn't much like it here, but she wouldn't have gone off without so much as a by-your-leave."

"Mr. Daggett is under the impression she went home," Witherspoon said softly.

"She didn't," Hortense insisted. "She wouldn't do something that daft. Besides, she left here with just her coat and hat on. How could she have paid her train fare?"

"We'll have the local police check to see if she's at her old home," Barnes said gently. "It won't take long before we've an answer." But he did find it odd that Daggett was so unconcerned about the girl's disappearance.

"Thank you, sir, I'd be ever so relieved to know that she was home safe. But I don't think that's where she's gone. I think something's happened to her." She shifted her gaze slightly, looking at someone who'd just come into the room. "Oh, Mrs. Benchley, the police are here. I'm telling them about Nelda being missing."

Witherspoon leapt to his feet as a woman with her head bandaged just above the left eye came into the dismal room. She stared at them for a moment, then said, "I'm Edith Benchley. I'm the housekeeper here."

"I'm Inspector Witherspoon and this is Constable Barnes."

"If you're through with Hortense, perhaps the girl can get back to her duties."

"We've no more questions at present." Witherspoon smiled kindly at the girl as she got to her feet. "I promise, we'll let you know as soon as we hear anything."

"Thank you, sir," Hortense replied gratefully. She gave the housekeeper a quick, rebellious glance. "I didn't know Nelda very long, but she was a nice girl. Didn't have much family to speak of, just an old aunt. But I don't think she run off home the way they're all sayin'."

"Did Nelda have a young man?" Constable Barnes asked.

Hortense hesitated for a split second. "There'd been a lad who walked her home from chapel a time or two."

"Chapel?" Witherspoon repeated.

"Nelda was a Methodist," Mrs. Benchley said. "And it was more than just a time or two. He's been walking her home every Sunday and he's escorted her to the park on her day out for the last month. So don't you be trying to fool the police into thinking we're a hard-hearted bunch that doesn't care a whit that a young woman in my charge has disappeared."

"I wasn't tryin' to do that, ma'am," Hortense protested. "But I overheard what Mr. Daggett was sayin' yesterday, and if Nelda ain't run off with Ian, then something's happened to her."

"Nothing's happened to her," Mrs. Benchley said calmly. "And you're not to blame Mr. Daggett for thinking she'd run home; that's what I told him. Now if you'll run along to the kitchen, I'd like to have a word with the police."

The woman's tone brooked no argument, so Hortense bobbed a quick curtsey and hurried away. As soon as she'd closed the door behind her, the housekeeper turned her attention to the two policemen. "I'm terribly sorry I haven't been able to speak with you until now, but I've been somewhat indisposed."

Witherspoon's gaze flicked to her bandage. "Uh, yes, we can see that. Er, uh, I take it you believe the girl's not come to any harm?"

Mrs. Benchley gave them a weary smile. "I don't think anything's happened to Nelda that she didn't want to happen. Oh, Inspector, it's all been a dreadful mess. I understand you're here investigating a murder, is that correct?"

"Right, a man named Harrison Nye was killed the night before last. From what we understand, Mr. Daggett was with him shortly before he died. As a matter of fact, Mr. Daggett had something so urgent to tell Mr. Nye, he interrupted a dinner party. Do you have any idea what that could have been?"

She shook her head. "I've no idea. Mr. Daggett wasn't in the habit of sharing information with his servants."

"We understand he'd been ill that day," Barnes said. "Hortense told us he'd been abed most of the day."

"That's correct. Dr. Wiltshire went up to see Mr. Daggett after he finished bandaging my head. I needed a few days' rest, and he wanted to be sure that Mr. Daggett understood that I wasn't to be on my feet. I don't know what happened, but Mr. Daggett left only moments after the doctor did. Later, we found out that he'd gone to see Mr. Nye and that Mr. Nye had been killed that night."

"Did you actually see Mr. Daggett leave?" Barnes asked.

"No, by that time I was abed myself." She smiled and lightly patted the bandage on her forehead. "But I got a detailed account of everything from our cook."

"I take it, then, you've no idea what time Mr. Daggett returned home that night?"

"I'm afraid not," she admitted. "As I said, I was sound asleep. But you might ask Clark—he generally stays up until Mr. Daggett comes home. He's our footman, and it's his task to make sure all the downstairs doors and windows are bolted."

The inspector nodded and made a mental note to speak to both Clark and the cook. He also decided that their next stop would be Dr. Wiltshire's surgery. He was very keen to know what the doctor had said to Mr. Daggett to send him running out into the night. "Thank you, Mrs. Benchley, we'll do that. Now, could you please provide us with Nelda Smith's home address? I did promise Miss Rivers that we'd see if the girl had indeed gone home."

"Certainly, I'll get it straightaway. But I'm fairly sure you'll find that she isn't there," Mrs. Benchley replied. "I think she's run off with her young man."

"We do need to check," Barnes said. "What's this lad's name and where does he live?" He was fairly sure the housekeeper would have that information. Most households kept a fairly tight rein on the young women who worked for them. Some places even forbade the girls to have outings with young men in case they'd fall in love, marry and leave their posts. But times had changed a bit since he was a young man. These days, there were more and more young women refusing to work in those sorts of households.

"His name is Ian Carr. He seems a respectable enough young man. He works on his family's barge. I believe he lives somewhere near the river, but I'm not sure. Mr. Daggett wasn't overly strict about such things, and I didn't feel it was my place to get every little detail from Nelda. She's generally a sensible young woman."

"So you don't think she's come to any harm?" Witherspoon persisted.

"Hardly, Inspector," she said with a knowing smile. "If I honestly thought Nelda had truly disappeared, I'd have been down to the police station straightaway."

Barnes studied her appraisingly. She stared back without flinching. Finally, he said, "You seem certain she's gone off with this young man, why?"

"Because I think she was fed up with Mr. Daggett." Mrs. Benchley sighed. "The poor girl had run her legs off that day. She'd changed his bed twice and taken him three clean nightshirts."

"But wasn't that her job?" Barnes commented.

"No, Constable. She was hired as a maid, not a nurse."

"But Mr. Daggett was ill . . ." the inspector pointed out.

"Nonsense, there wasn't a thing wrong with him except a little indigestion. Most of Mr. Daggett's ailments are in his head. He has the doctor around here at least twice a month." She pursed her lips and stood up. "Nelda had finally had enough. The last time she went into his room, he gave her some silly errand to run. It was dark, Inspector, and the girl doesn't know the city at all, but that didn't stop Mr. Daggett from sending her out on some silly errand. I think she went out, got a bit frightened, went and found her young man and he took her home. That's what I think and frankly, if I had a young man as good-hearted and handsome as hers dancing attendance on me, I wouldn't stay here one minute more than I had to."

The two policemen exchanged glances. "We'll certainly have a word with Mr. Daggett about that," the inspector said. "He never mentioned sending the girl out on an errand."

"I'm sure he didn't," Mrs. Benchley said coldly. "But that's precisely what he did. Feel free to question the rest of the household. They'll tell you the same thing."

"Thank you, ma'am." Witherspoon rose politely. "We would like a word with the rest of the servants, and do you know if Mr. Daggett is available?"

"Mr. Daggett's gone out. He didn't say where, but I do know he's planning on paying a condolence visit to Mrs. Nye this afternoon."

"I suppose this is as good a place to start as any," Betsy muttered to Wiggins. "But I'm not sure about this. It seems to me we're spreading ourselves very thin."

"It should be all right," Wiggins said easily. "It's like Mrs. Jeffries says, we've not really got much choice. There's a lot of territory to cover. We've got to suss out this Daggett fellow *and* the guests at the dinner party *and* the Nye household."

They were standing on a busy corner in South Kensington. Naturally, before their meeting this morning had broken up, they'd all changed their minds several times on what they were going to do next.

As it happened, they'd finally decided that Wiggins was going to snoop about for a housemaid or a footman from the Daggett household and Betsy was going learn what she could about the victim. Smythe had headed out on a mysterious errand of his own, Mrs. Jeffries had gone to Fulham to learn a bit more about the disappearing Miss Geddy and Luty had gone off with the list of names from the Nyes' dinner party. Hatchet had decided he wanted to find out a bit about Harrison Nye as well—he was very much of the opinion that the more one learned about the victim, the easier it was to find the killer.

Betsy agreed with that assessment too. She wasn't dragging her feet because she was annoyed at her assignment. She was miffed at her intended. He'd been far too vague about where he was going and what he was up to. She hated that. She worried about him as much as he worried about her, and he'd been overly casual when she'd asked him where he was off to this afternoon.

"Oh, 'ere and there," he'd said with a casual shrug of his big shoulders. But she'd not been fooled for a moment. He'd not been able to look her in the eyes, and that meant he was up to something. She knew he went to some dangerous places to do his investigating. Not that he couldn't take care of himself; he could. He was a strong man. But even the strongest man couldn't do much if someone shoved a knife in his back or coshed him over the head to steal his money.

"Are ya all right?" Betsy jumped as Wiggins screamed the question in her left ear.

"Stop shouting at me." She cuffed him in the arm. "Of course I'm all right."

"I've been talkin' to ya for five minutes and ya 'aven't answered. I thought you was fixin' to 'ave one of them fits or something." He gazed at her accusingly. "I was just tryin' to make sure you was all right."

Contrite, she smiled at him. "Oh, Wiggins, I'm sorry. My mind was elsewhere. I was woolgathering, and I didn't hear you. I'm fine. Now, I'm going to take myself off toward Belgrave Square and see if I can get a few shopkeepers to talk to me. Do you want to meet back here and we'll pop into that Lyon's up the road and have tea?"

He brightened immediately. "That sounds nice. I do love them hot cross buns they serve. I'll meet you right here at two o'clock." He gave her a jaunty wave and stepped off the curb.

"Be careful," she called after him, as he darted between a hansom and a cooper's van. She held her breath till he was safely on the other side of the busy road, then she turned and started off in the opposite direction. She hoped one of them found out something useful.

Wiggins spent a good part of the afternoon hanging about near the front of the Daggett house. He tried to be as inconspicuous as possible, but when he noticed the butler from the house across the street peering out the front window for the third time, he knew that his loitering had been noticed.

"Blow me for a game of tin soldiers," he muttered in disgust. But the game was up, and he knew he'd best take himself off. That nosy butler would be calling the police in two shakes of a lamb's tail, he knew that. Irritated with the wasted afternoon, Wiggins trudged off to his meeting with Betsy. He hoped Betsy and the others were having a better afternoon than he was.

Luty boldly marched up the walkway to the tall, elegant, town house on Ridley Square and banged the knocker. As the door opened, she plastered a huge smile on her face. A poker-faced butler stuck his head out and peered down at her. "Yes, madam, may I help you?"

"I'd like to see Mrs. Ryker, please. If she's at home. Here's my card." Luty gave him one of her calling cards.

He pulled the door open wider. "Please come inside, madam, and I'll see if Mrs. Ryker is receiving." He waved toward a tall-backed chair next to a round table with a gigantic fern sprouting out of a Chinese-style pot. "Please make yourself comfortable."

Luty nodded and sat down to wait. She'd just about had a stroke when she got a gander at that guest list from the Nye dinner party. Hilda and Neville Ryker were old friends of hers. She'd known them for years and even better, Hilda loved gossiping more than just about anything. The woman could talk the hair off a cat. She straightened as she heard footsteps coming down the hall. She smiled smugly, glad she hadn't told the others of the connection. They'd be real surprised when she told them about it at their next meeting.

"Mrs. Ryker is at home, madam," the butler said. "Right this way, please."

She followed him into a large, beautifully furnished drawing room. A tall, hawkish-looking woman with salt-and-pepper-colored hair, a long nose and a wide, thin mouth was sitting on a gold damask settee. "Goodness, Luty Belle, do come in. It's been ages since I've seen you. Do sit down, please."

"Howdy, Hilda, it has been a while." Luty sat down on a chair. "Sorry for bargin' in like this, but I was in the neighborhood and realized I'd not seen ya in quite a spell."

"Don't apologize." Hilda Ryker smiled widely, obviously delighted to see her friend. "I'm thrilled you've stopped in to call. It's been ages since we've had us a nice good gossip."

Luty chuckled. "You're a woman after my own heart. It has been too long. So, have ya done anything interestin' lately?"

" 'Interesting'? I should hope so!" Hilda's eyes sparkled. "You'll never guess what happened the other evening. I was at a dinner party, and the host was murdered."

"In front of everyone?" Luty pretended ignorance. Hilda wouldn't take kindly to figuring out that she'd only come around to get the goods on Harrison Nye. "Now that's what I'd call an interestin' party."

"No, no, no." Hilda waved her hand. "He was murdered later that night. In Fulham. He was stabbed. I'm surprised you haven't heard of it, it's been in all the papers."

"I've been too busy to read the papers," Luty replied.

"Well, go on, tell me the rest. Who was this fellow, and who killed him?"

"He's a business friend of Neville's." Hilda pursed her lips in disapproval. "His name's Harrison Nye. He's a bit of a mystery man, or I should say he was a bit of a mystery. He never spoke much about himself or where he'd come from."

Luty stared at Hilda. For all her wealth and breeding, she generally wasn't a snob. "You don't sound like you liked the fellow very much."

"I know one shouldn't speak ill of the dead," Hilda said, "and I'm sorry he was murdered; but honestly, I wasn't in the least surprised he was killed. He could be quite charming, you know, but only when it suited him. There was something cold about him."

"Ruthless sort, was he?" Luty prodded. She bided her time; she wasn't going to budge out of this chair until she got every last detail about that night out of Hilda.

"Very." Hilda leaned forward eagerly. "He's one of those businessmen who has his fingers in lots of different pies, if you know what I mean."

"And no one knows where he came from?" Luty pressed. "I mean, did he just show up in London with a fistful of cash and start buyin' up everything he wanted?"

"He wasn't quite that blatant. But he certainly managed to find opportunity everywhere he turned. As I said, I'm not surprised he was murdered. I suspect he was the sort that has lots of enemies. What was he doing in Fulham in the middle of the night? That's what I want to know. Mr. Ryker and I didn't leave the dinner party till almost ten-forty-five—that means he must have gone out after everyone had left."

"You were the last to leave?" Luty asked. Now they were getting somewhere. She wanted details about that night. She already knew Nye was shady as all get out.

"Lionel was still there." Hilda waved her hand. "He's Eliza's cousin."

"Eliza?"

"Mrs. Nye. She's a niece by marriage of Lord Cavan-augh." Hilda waved her arms expansively. "Actually, it was the most interesting dinner party I've been to in years. Halfway through the fish course, the butler came in and told Harrison he had a visitor who insisted on seeing him immediately. Naturally, Harrison told the butler not to be absurd, that he was with his guests. All of a sudden, the dining-room door flew open and this wild-eyed fellow burst into the room. We were all quite startled; Neville almost choked on his trout."

"What happened then?" Luty pressed. Hilda was easily distracted, and her favorite subject was her husband.

"That was the oddest part of all, as soon as Harrison laid eyes on the man, he leapt to his feet and the two of them disappeared. He didn't come back until Eliza went and reminded him that they had guests."

"So he came back to the table with his wife?" Luty asked.

"Not quite then. It was a few minutes later. I remember because he came back into the room with Lionel."

"Did he say anything when he came back?"

"Hardly." Hilda looked amused. "Harrison Nye had more arrogance than the Kaiser. He offered no apology. He simply sat down and started eating his charlotte russe."

"Do you know who the man was that come to see him?"

"His name was Daggett." Hilda grinned. "I didn't know who he was, but I overheard Lionel ask Eliza what the dickens that Daggett fellow was doing there. Those were his exact words."

"Did she know why he'd come?"

"Hadn't any idea at all. She just shrugged and kept that silly smile on her face. But you could tell she wasn't happy. Of course, that's understandable, no one likes having an important dinner party interrupted." Hilda laughed. "No one, of course, but the guests. It did liven the party up a bit. This fellow was terribly disheveled-looking. His hair was standing on end, his tie was askew and he was panting like he'd run for miles. Neville and I were ever so curious. That's one of the reasons we stayed so late. I had the impression something else was going to happen, and as it was, I was right."

Mrs. Goodge picked up the plate of scones and hurried back to the table. She was in luck today, her source not only talked a blue streak, she also might actually have something useful to say. The cook thanked her lucky stars that she'd had the good sense to ask her old friend Ida Leahcock to come round yesterday afternoon. Ida hadn't known anything about the case, but she'd known who might.

"If you're curious about that Nye murder, you might want to have a chat with Jane Melcher," Ida had said. "Her agency is just around the corner from there, and she's probably heard servant's gossip about the household." She'd taken Ida's advice and sent Jane Melcher a note yesterday evening inviting her around for morning tea. As she hadn't had any contact with the woman in over twenty-five years, she'd no idea if Jane Melcher would give her the time of day, much less come around for tea. But lo and behold, the woman had turned up right after breakfast.

"Here you are, Jane. You just help yourself now." The cook put the plate within easy reach of her companion and took her own seat.

Jane Melcher, a plump, gray-haired woman dressed in a dark aubergine-colored bombazine dress, helped herself to a scone. "It's been ages since we've seen each other." She picked up her knife and slit the scone in half. "I was ever so surprised to get your note. Nicely surprised, mind you. I said to Harriet, she's my typewriter girl, that I'd pop right along to see you. We shouldn't be too busy today, so Harriet will be all right on her own."

"Well, I do think old colleagues ought to keep in touch. Besides, I didn't know what had happened to you after I left Rolston Hall. I happened to run into Ida Leahcock a while back, and she mentioned you had your own business. I was ever so impressed."

"It's just a small domestic staffing agency," she replied.

"Don't be so modest. You ought to be very proud of yourself. Ida says you're very successful, that you find domestic staff for some of the best families in London." Mrs. Goodge firmly believed it never hurt to butter up your source before you pumped her for information.

Jane smiled modestly and stuck her knife in the butter dish. She slathered the top half of the scone. "I do my best. How is Ida these days?"

"She's doing quite well, not that you could tell by looking at her. She still dresses as plain as a pikestaff."

"She never was one to waste money. Maybe that's why she's got so much of it." Jane chuckled at her own witticism. "So how do you like your position here? You work for a policeman, I believe you said."

"He's an inspector," Mrs. Goodge retorted proudly. "Inspector Gerald Witherspoon. I'm surprised you haven't heard of him. He's quite a famous detective. He's solved ever so many cases. He's working on one right now. That man that was stabbed the other night in Fulham, that's his case." She held her breath, hoping Jane would take the bait. When the two women had worked together at Rolston Hall, Jane Melcher always had to be just that bit better than you. No matter what gossip you'd heard, she'd heard more. No matter where you went, she'd gone to someplace nicer and more expensive. No matter what you got for Christmas, she got something prettier. Mrs. Goodge sincerely hoped that old age hadn't improved Jane's character.

"Of course I've heard about that case." Jane smiled knowingly. "Actually, I heard all about it before it was even in the papers. One of the girls I placed as a kitchen maid in the house next door to the Nyes' came by early that morning and told me everything. My girls all know how I like to know what's what. Mind you, I'm not one to gossip, but one has a responsibility to know about the community when one is placing innocent young women in service."

"You never were one to gossip; but, of course, you've got to do your duty." Mrs. Goodge crossed her fingers under the table and silently prayed the Almighty would forgive her the lie.

"That's exactly how I see it," Jane nodded eagerly. "According to what Ellen told me, the night he was murdered, Mr. Nye scarpered off practically in the middle of a dinner party. His last guest hadn't even gone." She ate a bite of scone.

"You don't say." Mrs. Goodge nodded encouragingly.

"Shocking, it was. Absolutely shocking. But then again, Harrison Nye might have lived in that big house and been married to Lord Cavanaugh's niece, but he wasn't really top-drawer, if you know what I mean."

"Absolutely," the cook agreed. "He's probably one of those people who made their money in trade."

"Humph," Jane snorted, "or worse. He pretends to be a respectable businessman, but I say anyone as secretive as him must have something to hide. It was no surprise to me that he was murdered. Sins of the past catching up with him, that's what I say."

"Secretive? Gracious, that certainly doesn't sound very respectable." Mrs. Goodge had struck gold. All she had to do was keep Jane talking.

"Oh, it's the talk of the neighborhood." Jane waved her knife in emphasis. "He used to insist that his staff never say a word to anyone about his household. Instant dismissal if you were caught gossiping. What's so stupid is when you try that hard to stop talk, it just makes it worse."

"What kind of gossip is there?"

"The usual." Jane helped herself to another scone. "Mrs. Nye is a bit too friendly with that cousin of hers; Mr. Nye sneaks out in the middle of the night—that sort of thing. Mind you, I don't know if it's true."

"I take it her cousin is a man?" Mrs. Goodge asked.

"Lionel Bancroft."

"So, Mrs. Nye is too friendly with her cousin, eh?" Mrs. Goodge repeated. "I wonder if the police know that?"

"Why should they?"

"It was her husband that was murdered. If Mrs. Nye was in love with someone else . . ." She let her voice trail off meaningfully.

"I've already thought of that," Jane said briskly. "But neither of them could have done it. I know for a fact that Mrs. Nye retired for the evening right after the last guest left and Lionel Bancroft, who was the last guest that night, left after Harrison Nye had already gone."

"Maybe she slipped out the back way," Mrs. Goodge argued. She thought that a fairly unlikely scenario. One of the servants would have seen her leave, but she wanted to keep the information coming, and nothing loosened Jane's tongue like someone else appearing to know more than she did.

Jane shook her head stubbornly. "I don't think that's likely. How would Mrs. Nye have gotten to Fulham at that time of night?"

"By hansom."

"Ladies don't take hansom cabs at that time of night. It would be too easy to be noticed, and Eliza Nye would never do anything to be disgraced."

"She mustn't be too worried about disgrace if she's having a romp with her cousin," Mrs. Goodge retorted.

"Oh that's just talk." Jane shrugged dismissively. "She wouldn't pay any attention to that. But she certainly wouldn't have anything to do with murder. Not after what happened to her father. Why, it positively ruined the family."

Mrs. Goodge stared at her. "What did happen?"

"Her father murdered her mother, and then committed suicide. I'm amazed you don't remember it. It happened about twelve years ago. John Durney accused his wife of having an affair with their gardener. He shot her with one of his grandfather's dueling pistols, then turned the other gun on himself. The scandal ruined the girl's chance to make a decent match. That's probably why she married Harrison Nye. I expect her money had run out by the time he proposed."

CHAPTER 6

"Are you saying you haven't interviewed the widow properly?" Chief Inspector Barrows stared at Witherspoon from the other side of his desk.

"It was impossible, sir," Witherspoon explained. "She was quite hysterical. I meant to go back the first thing this morning, but a number of other things cropped up, and I didn't get the chance. Constable Barnes and I were on our way there when I received the message that you wanted to see me."

Barrows leaned back in his chair. "Look, Inspector, I'm not trying to tell you how to run this investigation, but it is customary to interview the victim's spouse as soon as possible after a murder."

"Yes, sir, I quite understand. But as I said, Mrs. Nye was hysterical." Witherspoon cocked his head to one side. "If you don't mind my asking, sir, I've often gone a day or two without questioning a spouse, and you've never objected before. I've always put that fact in my reports, I've never tried to hide it."

"I know. Normally, I wouldn't bother you with such

nonsense. But I was walking down the hall with the commissioner's private secretary when all of a sudden Inspector Nivens came rushing in waving an article from the *Policeman's Gazette*." Barrows sighed. "The article said what most policemen already know, that the most likely suspect in a murder is generally the victim's husband or wife. Well, the upshot of the whole business was Nivens managed to work it into the conversation that you were handling the Nye murder and had you interviewed Mrs. Nye yet? By that time Pomeroy, that's the commissioner's private secretary, decided to put his oar in the water and insisted it be done right away."

The inspector knew he wasn't very sophisticated when it came to Scotland Yard and Home Office politics, but he did rather suspect that this Pomeroy fellow and Inspector Nivens were good friends. He'd heard it said that Inspector Nivens was politically and socially very well connected. "As I said, sir, I was on my way to interview Mrs. Nye when I was called here."

Barrows gave a short, bark of a laugh. "Yes, I daresay you were. Now that you're here, you might as well report. How is the investigation going? Is there an arrest on the horizon?"

"It's a very complicated case, sir." Witherspoon frowned. "I don't think we'll be making any arrests just yet. We've a lot of territory to cover first. We think we've a good lead on finding out why Harrison Nye went to Fulham that night. That ought to help clear up the mystery a bit." He glanced at the clock on the wall behind Barrow's. "Er, is there anything else, sir? It's getting late."

"No," the chief inspector interrupted. "I've done my duty and had a word with you. I trust you'll keep me informed as to your progress."

"Yes, sir, certainly." He muttered a hasty good-bye and marched out of the office. Constable Barnes was waiting for him just outside the door. "Everything all right, sir?" Barnes inquired.

"I think so." Witherspoon found the entire episode

rather odd. "All he wanted to know was whether or not we'd interviewed Mrs. Nye."

Barnes's bushy eyebrows rose. "He drug us all the way up here to ask you that?"

Witherspoon looked over his shoulder as they headed for the stairs. He didn't want anyone to overhear him. "I don't think he had much choice. I'll tell you all about it as soon as we're outside."

They went down the stairs and crossed the foyer. As soon as they were safely out the door, Witherspoon told Barnes what had transpired in Barrows's office. The constable's eyes narrowed angrily, but he held his tongue.

"I do believe that Mr. Pomeroy and Inspector Nivens are friends," Witherspoon said. "I suspect that Nivens is a bit annoyed that he didn't get this case."

"He's as jealous as an old cat," Barnes said bluntly. He loathed Nivens as did just about every uniformed lad that had ever worked with the man. "You'd best watch yourself, sir. I think Nivens's resentment of you is getting worse."

"Oh dear, that will make things awkward," Witherspoon replied. He waved at a passing hansom. The driver spotted him and pulled over to the curb. "Do you think I ought to have a talk with him?" he asked as he climbed inside. "Take us to Upper Belgrave Street," he ordered the driver.

"I don't think that'd work, sir," Barnes replied as he slid into the seat next to the inspector. He grabbed the hand-rest as the cab started off.

"Really? Oh dear, that is a problem. I don't like to think that Inspector Nivens resents me."

"He does, sir." Barnes wanted to make sure this was understood. It was only a miracle that Nivens's constant undermining of the inspector hadn't already resulted in a transfer or demotion for Witherspoon. "And you can bet your last bob that it wasn't any accident that Nivens 'happened' to run into the chief inspector while he was with the chief."

Witherspoon stared at him over the top of his spectacles. "Are you saying you think the whole event was . . . er . . . orchestrated so that the chief would have reason to call me into his office?"

Barnes nodded. "That's exactly what I'm sayin', sir. It weren't exactly a reprimand, but it wasn't very nice, was it?"

"Not really."

Barnes took a deep breath and plunged ahead. He had to warn the inspector, had to make him understand how damaging Nivens could be. "He's a dangerous man, sir. He sees you as a threat to his climb to the top. He's desperate for power and position. He's not the least interested in justice, sir."

"That's a bit harsh, don't you think?"

"No sir, I don't. I've known the man since he come on the force and he got where he is today by bootlicking, undermining, tattling on his fellow officers and taking the credit for others' hard work. He's out to get you, sir. You'd best watch your back."

Witherspoon gaped at the constable. Barnes was a fair and honest man. He wouldn't make up lies about someone merely because he disliked that person. "But why? I've not done anything to him. Why would he want to harm my career?"

"Like I said, sir, you're a threat to him." Barnes sighed. "Your solving all these murders the last few years has pushed him farther and farther into the background. Before, when you were still working in the records room, most of the inspectors were all much the same. They had about the same number of good arrests and about the same percentage solving their cases. Inspector Nivens, with his political friends and his bootlickin' and backstabbing, tended to pull ahead of the pack a bit. Then you come along and solved them Kensington High Street killings and got started with solving just about every murder that come along. It made him look bad, sir, because it made him look ordinary."

Witherspoon was stunned. "It's not very pleasant thinking that someone dislikes me merely because I'm doing my duty."

Barnes winced as he saw the stricken expression on his superior's face. "You do a great deal more than your duty, sir, and that's what scares Nivens so much. I'm only tellin' you this so you'll keep your guard up, sir."

"I'm not sure I know how to do that," the inspector admitted honestly. "How can one defend oneself against innuendos and er . . . what did you call it, 'backstabbing'?"

"You can't, sir," Barnes said honestly. "But you can fire off a few salvos on your own."

"I'm not sure I understand what you mean." He looked out the side as the hansom pulled up in front of the Nye house.

"For starters," Barnes said as he jumped down, "you can complain to Barrows about Nivens interferin' with your investigation."

Witherspoon handed the driver some coins. "But he hasn't done that."

"Sure he has," Barnes said cheerfully. "Several of the lads who did the house-to-house in Fulham said they spotted Nivens snooping about and what's more, he pulled Constable Peters aside and started questioning him."

"Gracious, really. He did all that?" Witherspoon marched up the walkway toward the house.

"He did, sir, and if you complain to Barrows, that'll get Nivens off your patch for a good while. He's not just a greedy little sod, sir. He's a coward too. It'll scare the daylights out of him to get called on the carpet for stickin' his nose in where it don't belong."

Witherspoon thought about what Barnes told him as they went into the Nye house and waited for the butler to announce them. He was terribly confused. The very idea of running to the chief inspector and complaining about another officer was repugnant to him. Yet he trusted Constable Barnes implicitly, and if he said that Nivens was out to damage him, Witherspoon couldn't ignore the situation. Besides, if he were really truthful with himself, finding out that Nivens was out to do him a disservice was certainly no surprise. He'd never been more than barely civil to Witherspoon. But the inspector had always told himself Nivens's surliness was merely his nature and that it wasn't personal. It seems now that he was wrong. Nivens was out to destroy his career. He took that quite personally indeed.

"If you'll come this way, gentlemen." Duffy's words interrupted his reveries. "Mrs. Nye is receiving in the drawing room."

They followed him down the hallway. Eliza Nye, dressed in widows' black, rose from where she'd been sitting on the settee. A tall, fair-haired man of about thirty-five was in the room with her. "Hello, Inspector, Constable," she said softly. "This is my cousin, Lionel Bancroft."

Both policemen nodded politely, then Witherspoon focused his attention on Mrs. Nye. Her eyes were red and swollen from crying, her face was pale and she had a decidely haggard air of grief about her. It was difficult to see such a sad, delicate creature as a murderess, but the inspector knew that even the sweetest countenance could mask the heart of a monster. Still, he didn't think she'd be so upset if she'd murdered her husband. "Again, Mrs. Nye, please accept our condolences on the loss of your husband. We'll do everything in our power to bring his killer to justice."

"Thank you, Inspector." She smiled weakly. "I'm sure you will. Let's all sit down. You must have a number of questions to ask me."

"Are you certain you're up to this, my dear?" Lionel Bancroft patted her hand.

"I must," she replied. "Regardless of how distressing it is." She sat back down. Her cousin took the spot next to her.

"We'll do our best to make this as painless as possible," Witherspoon said, as he and Barnes sat down on the opposite love seat. He thought he might as well start with the most obvious questions. "Do you know of anyone who would want to harm Mr. Nye?"

"No, Inspector. I can't think of anyone who would wish him ill."

"He hadn't any enemies? Disgruntled business associates, uh, staff that have been let go . . ."

"He was a businessman, Inspector." She shrugged slightly. "Sometimes quite a ruthless one at that, but as far as I know, no one ever threatened him."

"Would he have told you if he had been in fear of his life?" Barnes asked softly.

She hesitated briefly. "Truthfully, I'm not sure. Harrison was very protective of me."

"Of course he wouldn't have told you such a thing," Bancroft interjected. "He would never have worried you like that." He looked at the policemen, his expression grim. "Mrs. Nye doesn't wish to speak ill of her husband."

"Lionel," she yelped. "What on earth are you doing?"

"I'm telling them the truth, my dear. I don't wish to cause you pain, but if the police are going to find out who killed Harrison, they need to know the truth about him."

"And what would that be, sir?" Witherspoon asked quickly. He didn't want Mrs. Nye stopping her cousin from talking. Sometimes it was unexpected outbursts like these that gave one the very clue one needed to solve the case.

Lionel shot his cousin a quick, beseeching glance, then said, "Unfortunately, Harrison had a lot of enemies. Why, even some of the people who were having dinner here the night of the murder would have wished him dead."

"Lionel, please," Mrs. Nye pleaded. "You mustn't say such things. It's not true. Harrison had made his peace with those two."

"Perhaps it would be easier on Mrs. Nye if we spoke with you alone?" Barnes suggested.

"No," she yelped. Then she appeared to get ahold of herself and took a long, deep breath. She smiled wanly at her cousin. "Lionel, I know you're trying to spare my feelings, but I'd really rather cooperate with the police. The only way I shall ever sleep again is to know the police are doing their best to catch my husband's killer." She looked at Witherspoon. "I'm quite all right, Inspector. Please, do go on with your questions."

"Well, er, now that Mr. Bancroft's brought it up, perhaps he can elaborate on what he meant."

Lionel shot Eliza Nye one quick, anxious glance and then said, "As I said, Inspector, there were two people here who might have had a grudge against Harrison."

"And who would they be, sir?" Barnes asked quickly.

"His former solicitors, John and Peter Windemere."

The inspector looked at Eliza Nye. "Is this true?"

"I'm afraid it is, Inspector." She sighed. "Harrison had a property matter some years ago that they were handling for him. Unfortunately, they mishandled the sale so completely, the deal fell apart. It cost my husband an enormous amount of money. He sued them and was granted damages. It bankrupted the firm."

"Then why'd they come to dinner?"

"My husband asked me to invite them, Inspector. I've no idea why."

Witherspoon frowned slightly. "Didn't you find it strange that Mr. Nye would ask you to invite people who probably had a real reason to dislike him?"

"I didn't think it strange at all," she replied. "I only found out that they had reason to dislike my husband after they arrived that night."

Barnes asked. "Who told you?"

"My husband," she said. "We were just getting ready to come down when Duffy let them in and took them into the drawing room. They were the first guests to arrive. We were standing at the top of the stairs. I started to go down, but Harrison grabbed my arm and told me to wait. He was laughing. He said he wanted them to squirm for a few minutes. I asked him what on earth he was talking about. He told me what had happened years earlier. I was appalled, Inspector."

"Yes, I imagine that would have been a bit of a shock. Er," he hesitated, not quite certain what to ask next but knowing he ought to ask something. "Did your husband offer you an explanation as to why he wanted them at dinner? Forgive me, ma'am, but your description of your husband's behavior doesn't sound like he wanted to make peace with these men."

"No, it doesn't, does it? I suppose that now that Harrison's dead, I'd like to think him a better man than he was." She smiled sadly. "He said he invited them because he had a business proposal that might interest them."

"What kind of proposal?" Barnes asked.

"He didn't say. I was going to ask him about it later that evening, but as I'm sure you realize . . ." Her voice trailed off and her eyes filled with tears. "I never got the chance."

"How did they greet your husband?" Witherspoon thought that a good question. If someone had bankrupted him, he probably wouldn't have been very nice to him. Mind you, he couldn't imagine accepting a dinner invitation from the person responsible for ruining you.

"I don't know, Inspector," she admitted. "As we reached the bottom of the stairs, other guests were arriving, and I went to greet them. Harrison went on into the drawing room."

"I arrived about then with the Rykers," Lionel Bancroft interjected.

"I see." Witherspoon nodded. "Er, how were they all acting when you and your other guests arrived in the drawing room?"

"They weren't there," she said. "Harrison had taken them, and they'd disappeared into his study. They didn't come back until it was almost time for dinner. There didn't seem to be anything wrong. Everyone appeared very cordial. They weren't particularly talkative, but they weren't rude. All the other guests had arrived by then, so Harrison made the introductions."

"It was all very civilized, Inspector," Lionel added. "I'd no idea Harrison had been at odds with any of his guests until Eliza told me the next day. I do think you ought to question these men. If anyone had reason to dislike Harrison, I'm sure it was they."

"We shall have a word with both those gentlemen, I assure you," Witherspoon replied. His head was beginning to hurt a little. This case, which was already complicated, had just been made worse. He hadn't really considered the guests at the dinner party to be suspects. Apparently, he'd been wrong.

"Your husband seems to have spent most of that evening in his study instead of at the dining table," Barnes observed dryly.

Eliza Nye's perfect brow furrowed in confusion. "Oh yes, of course, you're referring to Oscar Daggett's peculiar outburst."

"The man has no manners whatsover," Lionel exclaimed. "He's another one you ought to have a word with."

"We have already spoken to Mr. Daggett," Witherspoon said. "Mrs. Nye, had you ever seen Daggett before that night?"

"Not often," she said. "But he's been here a few times. He and my husband used to be in business together but it was a long time ago."

"They aren't in business now?" the inspector pressed. Oscar Daggett had definitely implied he'd come to the Nye house about a business question.

"No."

"Are you absolutely certain of that?" Witherspoon wanted to be sure.

"Of course I'm sure," she said, her tone just a shade sharp.

"Really, Inspector," Lionel added. "I do believe Mrs. Nye knows who her husband does business with."

"She didn't know about the Windemere brothers' business relationship with her husband," Barnes said calmly.

"That was different," she snapped. "They hadn't had anything to do with Harrison in eleven years. He'd have hardly been likely to mention them, would he?"

Witherspoon decided to try a different tactic. "Your butler gave me the names of everyone who was at your dinner party. I understand Mr. Bancroft was the last to leave that night?"

"I was," Lionel admitted. "I stayed to have a word with Mrs. Nye. I left a few minutes after Harrison did."

"And I retired for the night right after Lionel left," Eliza Nye added.

"Yes, ma'am, we know that. We've already had a word with your staff. Your butler confirmed everyone's movements. Did your husband happen to mention where he was going when he left here?"

"He did not," she replied, "and I was rather annoyed with him about it. Of course I was careful not to show my displeasure in front of our guests."

"I understand he often left the house late at night," Witherspoon persisted.

"Often isn't the word I'd use, Inspector. When we were first married, he went out a time or two. When he saw how much it upset me, he stopped," she said. "Or if he left the house at night, he waited until after I'd retired for the evening."

"But he didn't that night, did he?" Barnes pointed out. "As a matter of fact, he left even before your last guests."

"I was going to speak to him about it later," she snapped. "But I never got the chance."

Mrs. Jeffries stood at the head of the table and double-checked to make sure everything was ready for tea. The others would be back soon, and she had no doubt they had much to discuss.

Mrs. Goodge came out of the dry larder carrying a loaf of plain brown bread. "There's a hot pot in the oven for

supper tonight, so I think all we need for tea this afternoon
is some bread and butter."

"Are any of the others back yet?" Mrs. Jeffries asked.

"I think I hear Luty and Hatchet pulling up outside."

"Betsy's here. She dashed upstairs to change the inspector's linens. The laundry boy is due by this evening."
Mrs. Goodge sincerely hoped the kitchen would be empty
by then—that lad was fairly sharp. She wanted to have a
moment or two alone to question him and see if he knew
anything useful.

"I'm all done." Betsy, her arms loaded with crumpled
sheets, hurried over to the wicker laundry basket sitting
beside the pine sideboard. She dumped the sheets inside.
"Shall I close it?"

"That's the last," Mrs. Jeffries replied. "Can you let
Luty and Hatchet in the back door?"

Betsy nodded and dashed off down the hall just as
Smythe came down the back stairs. "Where's she going?"
he asked the housekeeper.

"To let in Luty and Hatchet," Mrs. Goodge said.
"Where's Wiggins?"

"He's right behind me." Smythe slid into his usual
chair. "And from the expression on 'is face, I'd say he's
not got much to report."

The others came into the kitchen in a pack, with Luty
and Betsy in the lead. "Wait'll you hear what I found out,"
the elderly American exclaimed.

"You're not the only one who learned something useful," Hatchet added. As they'd reached the table, he pulled
out Luty's chair and seated her with a flourish. Betsy
dropped into the seat next to Smythe and gave him a
swift, intimate smile. She was still a bit annoyed that he'd
not told her where he went today, but she'd forgiven him.

"I've not found out anything." Wiggins dropped into
his seat. He looked hopefully at the plate of bread and
butter in the center of the table. Mrs. Goodge shoved it
toward him.

"Don't take it so hard, lad," Smythe said. "My day

wasn't all that good either." He'd gone to every dirty pub on the eastern docks and he'd not seen hide nor hair of his source, Blimpey Groggins. No one else had seen the man lately either. Smythe was a little concerned. It wasn't like Blimpey to pull a disappearing act like this. Bad for business it was.

"Iffen it's all the same to you, then, can I tell ya what all I learned?" Luty asked.

Mrs. Jeffries glanced around the table, saw no objections, then nodded. "Please, go ahead." She began pouring cups of tea.

Luty smiled delightedly. "Well, since you-all kindly let me have a look at that guest list, I gotta tell ya, I hit pay dirt."

Hatchet raised his eyebrows. "I take it that means you recognized at least one name on the list? Humph," he snorted, "no wonder you changed your mind about what you wanted to do."

"Don't be such a grouch." Luty grinned. "You'd have done the same. Besides, we change our minds all the time about what we're doin' and where we're goin' to be snoopin'."

"So you recognized a name on the list," Mrs. Jeffries prompted. Sometimes these two could waste an inordinate amount of time squabbling like children. "Do go on . . ."

"I decided I'd have a chat with my friend Hilda Ryker. Nice woman, likes to gossip and doesn't give herself airs. She was at the dinner party that night." Luty laughed. "Hilda said she'd only gone because her husband insisted. She didn't particularly care for Harrison Nye, and she didn't like his wife much either."

"Did she tell you why?" Mrs. Jeffries asked.

"I asked her, and she said she wasn't sure." Luty shrugged and reached for her cup of tea. "She couldn't rightly put her finger on why she didn't like 'em, she said she just didn't feel comfortable around either of 'em."

"But she didn't give any specific reason for her feelings?" Hatchet pressed. Sometimes, when madam was vague, it was because she was trying to keep a useful clue all to herself.

"No, like I said, she just didn't like 'em much. But, luckily, she went because Neville wanted her to and she said it ended up bein' one of the most interestin' evenin's she'd had in a long while. Oscar Daggett weren't the only interestin' distraction at that party." She paused dramatically. "The Windemere brothers was at the dinner party."

"Oh dear," Mrs. Jeffries exclaimed. "I meant to tell everyone their names were on the list, but it slipped my mind."

"It slipped your mind?" Betsy repeated incredulously.

"If you'll recall, we ended up in a rather heated argument at our last meeting," Mrs. Jeffries said defensively. "Between trying to determine who had how many cases to their credit and everyone changing their minds about what they were going to do next, I simply didn't think to mention it till everyone had gone. You all did leave rather quickly."

"That's all right, Hepzibah." Luty smiled smugly. "No harm was done. But like I was sayin', they was there that night, big as life. John Windemere sat right next to Hilda. She said you could tell by the way they was actin' that they was upset about something. Every time someone tried to start a conversation, they'd give a one-word answer or mumble something silly. Hilda said it was obvious to anyone who had half a brain that they didn't want to be there. To top it off, when Oscar Daggett come chargin' in lookin' as wild-eyed as a crazy coyote, the two brothers started grinnin' like a couple of fools."

"They knew Oscar Daggett?" Mrs. Jeffries asked.

"Hilda didn't think so," Luty replied. "As a matter of fact, she was sure they didn't. She overheard one of 'em say to the other that Daggett looked like trouble for Nye; he didn't use Daggett's name of course, just said 'the man.' The other one said he hoped so too."

"They were talking like that in front of Mrs. Nye?"

Mrs. Goodge looked at Luty over the top of her spectacles.

"She didn't hear 'em." Luty reached for a slice of bread. "One of the other guests had distracted everyone by gettin' up and leavin' the table. I, uh, think he went to the water closet."

"The water closet? That's an odd thing to do during a dinner party." Mrs. Goodge shook her head. "But then it sounds as if it was a very odd party to begin with."

"You can say that again," Luty said. "Hilda said it was the best one she's been to in years."

Mrs. Jeffries thought about what she'd just heard. It was, indeed, a very strange dinner party. "I wonder why Nye invited them?" she murmured.

"Maybe Mrs. Nye invited 'em," Wiggins suggested. As he didn't have anything useful in the way of information to contribute tonight, he felt duty-bound to ask good questions.

"That's a good question," the housekeeper agreed. "Why don't you see if you can find out the answer?"

Wiggins brightened. "You think it's important?"

She didn't, but as he wasn't doing very well in this investigation, she didn't want to discourage the lad. "Absolutely. See if you can find a servant from the household that might know who put the names on the guest list," she replied. "Now, who would like to go next?"

"I'll go next," Hatchet said. He paused for a brief moment, then plunged right ahead, determined not to let the madam's dramatic revelations bother him in the least. "It wasn't easy finding out anything about Frieda Geddy. But I persisted and did find out a few interesting tidbits." He took a quick sip of tea. "Frieda Geddy spoke Dutch."

"Dutch?" Mrs. Goodge frowned. "You mean she was a foreigner."

"No, I mean she spoke Dutch as a second language," he explained. "Her parents were Dutch."

"They were immigrants from the Netherlands?" Mrs. Jeffries clarified.

"No, no, I'm sorry, I'm not explaining this very well."
He took a deep breath. "Her mother was English and her
father was from someplace in Southern Africa, some place
near Johannesburg. My source wasn't exactly sure, but he
did know that Miss Geddy spoke Dutch and that she'd
learned it from her father."

"So maybe she was mailin' all them packages off to
South Africa," Wiggins suggested. "You know, sendin'
mittens and nice things off to her old dad."

"Her father died fifteen years ago," Hatchet said. "He
was killed in an accident in the Transvaal."

"Gracious, Hatchet, you have learned a lot." Mrs. Jeffries was rather impressed. "How on earth did you find
that out?"

Hatchet gave his mistress a quick, smug grin. He
wouldn't admit to anyone, least of all her, that he'd found
a former cleaning woman of Frieda Geddy's and bribed
her shamelessly. "Oh, I have my ways." He gave an ex-
aggerated sigh. "I only wish I could have learned more."

"What did her family do?" Mrs. Goodge asked.

"My source wasn't certain. She thought perhaps Miss
Geddy's family might have been in mining."

Mrs. Jeffries thought about that for a moment. "Did you
find out anything else?"

"No." Hatchet's shoulders slumped a bit. "I know we
need to find a connection between Miss Geddy and Harrison Nye, but honestly, I'm beginning to think there isn't
one."

"But there has to be," Betsy insisted. "He was on his
way to visit her; he must have been."

"He was murdered on her front steps," Smythe added.
"In the middle of the bloomin' night. There has to be a
connection."

"But no one I spoke to had any idea how they could
possibly be related," Hatchet argued. "Miss Geddy had no
friends or acquaintances in common with Nye, she certainly didn't travel in his social circle and as far as I can
see, she had no reason whatsover to have anything to do

with the man. The fact that she's disappeared and he's died doesn't necessarily mean the two of them have any connection with each other. After all, her disappearance took place two months before he got stabbed on her doorstep. It could very well be a coincidence."

Everyone thought about that for a moment. Then Wiggins said, "Maybe 'e went there that night because 'e knew that her house was goin' to be empty."

"How would he know that?" Mrs. Goodge frowned at the footman over the rim of her spectacles.

"Maybe 'e owns the 'ouse," Wiggins suggested. "We've 'eard that 'e owns lots of things, 'as his fingers in a lot of pies so to speak. Maybe he owns the freehold where she lives and when she didn't pay 'er rent, 'e knew the place was empty."

Again, there was a silence as everyone thought about Wiggins's observation.

"Cor blimey, the lad might be right," Smythe finally said. "Maybe he was goin' there to meet someone he didn't want to be seen with in public. What better place than a 'ouse he knew was empty."

"That's certainly possible," Mrs. Jeffries murmured. "If he was, indeed, the landlord, he'd have sent his agents around to collect the rent."

"He'd also have a key," Luty said softly. "Let's ask the inspector if they found a key on the body."

"I will," she replied thoughtfully. "Wiggins has raised a very interesting possibility. We need to find out if Harrison Nye had any way of knowing that house would be empty."

"I don't think it's likely," Mrs. Goodge said bluntly. "I think you're leapin' in the dark here. To begin with, we don't know that Nye does own that house, and even if he did, why go all the way to Fulham to meet someone. If he wanted privacy, he could have gone out into the middle of Belgrave Square. That time of night, there'd be no one about to see him. Besides, from everything we've heard, it was Oscar Daggett's visit that night that sent Nye out in the first place. How would he have had time to make any arrangements about meetin' someone in an empty house?"

Mrs. Jeffries smiled sheepishly. "Of course you're right. We are leaping in the dark as you say. But Wiggins does have a point. Nye's going to Fulham may have had nothing to do with Miss Geddy. We'll just have to keep investigating."

"Can I tell what I've found out?" the cook asked. "I think it's pretty interestin'." At the housekeeper's nod, she continued. "I found out a bit about Mrs. Nye today. It seems there's a bit of gossip about the area about her and her cousin, Lionel Bancroft. Some say they're a bit too friendly, even for family."

"You mean they're . . . uh"—a deep blush crept up Wiggins's cheeks—"sweethearts?"

"That's a polite way of sayin' it." Luty chuckled.

"That's one way of puttin' it." The cook tried to keep her expression stern, but it was hard. Sometimes she was amazed at how naive these young people were. "And that's not all I heard. Eliza Nye before she married was Eliza Durney. She's most definitely from one of the best families in England, her mother was Lord Cavanaugh's sister and her father, John Durney, was cousin to minor nobility on his mother's side. But Eliza's chances for a good match were ruined. There was a terrible scandal a few years ago. Her father found out his wife was having an"—she hesitated, trying to pick the least offensive word—"assignation with the gardener."

"Assignation," Wiggins interrupted as he scratched his chin. "What's that?"

"She were playin' about where she hadn't ought to be playin' about," Luty said quickly. "Go on," she urged the cook. "This is getting right interestin'."

Wiggins kept silent. He wasn't exactly sure what an assignation was, but he had a good idea. Nonetheless, he resolved to find out for certain from Smythe when the two of them were alone.

"Right"—the cook bobbed her head—"and in the middle of this . . . uh, assignation, Durney burst into his wife's bedroom and shot both Mrs. Durney and, of course, the gardener."

"Cor blimey." Smythe shook his head in disbelief. "Caught 'em in the act, did 'e?"

"And killed them," Mrs. Goodge said. "Then he turned the gun on himself. Eliza Nye found their bodies. No one else was home that day."

Wiggins was suddenly sure he knew exactly what they were talking about.

CHAPTER 7

Mrs. Jeffries slowly climbed the back stairs. She had much to think about. The evening was quickly drawing in but she was fairly confident the inspector wouldn't be home for a good while yet. Luty and Hatchet had gone home, Wiggins and Smythe were doing a few chores and Betsy was helping the cook finish the preparations for supper.

She stopped at the back-hall closet and took out the big ostrich-feather duster then she made her way to the drawing room. Sometimes she thought more clearly when she was doing a dull, boring task.

She turned on a lamp against the dim light. She walked over to the sideboard and ran the duster along the top. Their meeting had been very productive, and they'd learned a great deal of information. But what did it all mean?

From what they knew thus far, no one appeared to be overly fond of Harrison Nye. His former solicitors had no reason to wish him well that was for certain. He'd ruined their business. But why wait eleven years to take vengeance? Then again, they were solicitors, and waiting such a long time would make the police less likely to view them as suspects than if they'd murdered him when he'd ruined them. She finished dusting the sideboard and made her way to the table near the window. There were still so many unanswered questions. Why had Oscar Daggett interrupted the dinner party? What had happened that had made him leap out of a sickbed and rush over to see an old business partner? She made a mental note to find out if Daggett had received any visitors or messages prior to his going to Nye's house that night.

She finished dusting the furniture, then plopped down on a chair. All their cases tended to be complex, but this one seemed particularly puzzling. She wasn't sure why . . . then she realized it was probably because they had very little information about the victim. Who was Harrison Nye and, more importantly, why would someone hate him enough to kill him? Apparently, he'd quite a reputation as a ruthless businessman—that generally tended to make one unpopular. But there were many such men in London, and most of them didn't get murdered. Maybe they ought to look closer to home—it was certainly not unknown for a wife to want to rid herself of an inconvenient husband. Could it have been Mrs. Nye? According to what the cook had found out, there was ample evidence that Eliza Nye was in love with her cousin and had only married Nye because she needed money. Money was most definitely one of the more usual motives for murdering one's spouse.

But they'd no evidence that Eliza Nye had left the house that night. Beside, how would she have gotten to Fulham? Mrs. Jeffries knew full well that between the inspector's official investigation and Smythe's unofficial one, every hansom cab driver in the area had been questioned thoroughly. So far, none of them had mentioned taking a woman fitting Eliza Nye's description to Fulham.

The case was a puzzle, but Mrs. Jeffries was sure they'd solve it eventually. They generally did.

• • •

Even though it was past six o'clock, Dr. Douglas Wiltshire was still at his surgery when the inspector and Barnes arrived. "I'll be with you in a moment," Wiltshire called over his shoulder. He was at a sink on the far side of the examination room scrubbing his hands. "Please seat yourselves. There are chairs in my office."

The two policemen walked past the leather examination table to the small office adjacent to the surgery. They sat down on the two chairs in front of the doctor's simple wooden desk. Witherspoon wrinkled his nose at the harsh smell of disinfectant.

A tall, glass-fronted cupboard filled with bottles, vials and some rather frightening-looking instruments was on one side of the room. The opposite wall was covered with floor-to-ceiling bookcases, most of them medical texts. "I say, he's got rather a lot of books."

"And I use all of them," Dr. Wiltshire said as he came into the room. "There's discoveries being made every day in the medical field, and one has to keep up. The more I know, the better a doctor I can be. Sorry to keep you waiting, gentlemen." He sat down and gave them a friendly, if puzzled smile. "What can I do for you? Neither of you look ill."

"We're here to see you about one of your patients, sir," Witherspoon said. "We've a few questions for you."

"About my patient?" Wiltshire frowned. "I don't know that I'm at liberty to discuss anyone's medical condition without their permission. . . ."

"It's not really his medical condition we're concerned about," Witherspoon interrupted. "It's about Oscar Daggett, sir, and it's in connection with a murder investigation." He'd found that frequently people tended to loosen their tongues a bit when they knew the kind of crime the police were trying to solve.

"Daggett?" Wiltshire snorted. "The only thing wrong with him is he eats too much, exercises too little and takes himself far too seriously. He's got more aches and pains than an entire ward at the infirmary, and all of them are in his head!"

"But you were at his house on October 15," Witherspoon said. "Why did you go if he wasn't ill?"

"I was there twice that day," Wiltshire replied. "Once for him and once for his housekeeper. I go, Inspector, because the fool pays me well. I charge him double my usual fee."

"Double?" Witherspoon was rather shocked. It was rare that someone actually admitted to such a thing.

"Oh yes, patients like Daggett make it possible for me to give my services free of charge to the poor. Once a fortnight I work a clinic in the East End. But you're not here to talk about me. You want to know about Daggett. What can I say? There wasn't a thing wrong with the fellow that day. As usual, Daggett ate far too much at dinner the night before and had a case of indigestion. A simple dose of baking soda would have been adequate treatment for him, but he always sends one of his servants trotting over to fetch me." Wilshire rolled his eyes heavenward. "I've been to attend the fellow three times in the last fortnight, Inspector, and I was heartily sick of it. I had a look at him, ascertained his medical needs were minimal, then had a nice natter with his housekeeper about my dying orange tree. Later that evening, I was called back to attend Mrs. Benchley. She was actually in need of my services. Poor woman had a concussion."

"How was Mr. Daggett when you went back the second time?" Barnes said. "I believe you went up to see him."

"Oh yes, Mrs. Benchley was very worried that Mr. Daggett would be angry with her for needing to stay in bed. I assured her I'd have a word with him about how important it was she stay off her feet." He shook his head. "Actually, that's the only time I was ever seriously worried about Daggett."

"How do you mean, sir?" Barnes asked. He rather liked the doctor.

Wiltshire frowned thoughtfully. "When I got up to Daggett's room, he was still in bed. Before I could even tell him why I was there, he started moaning about how it wasn't fair, that I ought to have told him he was dying because a fellow needed time to get his affairs in order. I asked him what he was talking about and repeated my earlier diagnosis that there was nothing wrong with him but indigestion."

"From what you've told us about Mr. Daggett," Barnes said, "it sounds as if he always thought he was at death's door."

"That's quite true, Constable. But this time was different. He was convinced I'd come back for the deathwatch and that he was dying within the hour. I finally asked him where he got such a notion . . ." Wiltshire broke off with a sheepish smile. "And it turns out that he thought he was dying because he overheard me and Mrs. Benchley talking about my orange tree and how it was dying. He thought we'd been talking about him."

Witherspoon leaned forward in his chair. "Did he believe you?"

"Oh yes," Wiltshire said. "He knew I was speaking the truth. That's why I was so surprised by what happened next."

"What was that?" Barnes prodded.

"He leapt out of bed and began dressing. But what was so stunning is that was the first time since I've been treating the man that he actually looked ill. I got quite worried about him. All the color drained from Daggett's face, his eyes bulged like they were going to pop out of his head and he was in such a hurry to get me out of his room, he practically shoved me out the door." The doctor shook his head in disbelief. "He wouldn't even let me take his pulse or check his temperature."

Witherspoon wasn't sure he understood. "Let me make sure I understand what it is you're telling us. Daggett's demeanor changed dramatically after you told him he wasn't going to die?"

"That's right." Wiltshire smiled faintly. "Believe me, I

know it sounds ridiculous. Knowing the fellow as I do, I'd have predicted that upon learning he wasn't going to die, he'd have been dancing for joy. But honestly, Inspector, it was at that moment when the fellow looked the worst I've ever seen him."

Smythe knew that Betsy wasn't going to be pleased with the way he'd crept out of the house this evening, but he simply had to find out what was keeping Blimpey Groggins from his usual haunts. He pulled his coat tight against the chill night air and headed across the darkened communal gardens to the back gate. Smythe unlocked the gate, pulled it open and stepped out onto Edmonton Gardens. Within a few minutes, he was flagging down a hansom on Holland Park Road. "The West India Dock, please," he told the driver as he leapt into the seat. "And there's an extra shilling in it for ya if ya get me there quick."

They made it to the river in record time. "Where do you want to be let off?" the driver called over his shoulder.

"Anywhere along the waterfront will do." Smythe dug some coins out of his coat pocket. A few moments later, he swung out of the cab, paid the driver and headed across the road toward his destination.

Opening the door of the Artichoke Tavern, Smythe stepped inside and paused for a moment so his eyes could adjust to the smoky room. The scent of beer and gin mixed with tobacco smoke and unwashed bodies. Smythe spotted his quarry across the room.

She spotted him at the same time. Lila Clair met his gaze steadily as he made his way through the crowded room. She was a tall, black-haired woman in her fifties, her eyes were deep set, dark blue and had seen more than their fair share of misery. She was sitting at a table with three other girls. As the big man approached, she jerked her head sharply and the girls immediately got up.

"Hello, Smythe." She spoke first. "Funny seein' you here. This isn't your sort of place."

"May I 'ave a seat?" he asked. If he wanted her help, he knew he'd better treat her with respect.

She nodded. "You can buy me a drink if you've a mind to." Without waiting for his answer, she signaled the barmaid. "Bring us another," Lila called to the woman, "and a whiskey for the big fellah here."

Smythe didn't like whiskey, but he wanted her help, so he'd drink what she ordered. "I'm lookin' for Blimpey," he said.

Lila made a great show of gazing about the crowded room. "I don't see him 'ere," she finally said.

The drinks arrived. Smythe paid and picked up his glass. He downed the stuff in one big gulp.

Lila laughed. "You don't like it, do ya?"

"Not really," he admitted. "But as you'd taken the trouble to order it, I thought I'd better have a go. Look, I don't 'ave a lot of time . . ."

"Why'd you come 'ere?" she asked calmly. She took a sip of gin and stared at him steadily over the rim of her glass. "I'm not Blimpey's keeper."

"No, but you're the one that'd know if 'e was in trouble or something," he blurted. "You're about the only person on the face of the earth that Blimpey trusts, and I've got some work for 'im."

She studied him for a moment, then she grinned. "Is it important?"

"Very."

"Ya 'ave money?"

"I wouldn't come to see Blimpey without it."

She tossed back the last of her gin and rose to her feet. "Come on, then. I'll take ya to 'im." She laughed. "He'll not be pleased. He didn't want anyone to see him, but you're a good customer."

"Thanks, Lila." Smythe finished off the whiskey and got up. "I appreciate you takin' the trouble to 'elp me."

"You're a good man, Smythe." Lila smiled wearily.

"Some say you and your friends 'ave kept the coppers from arrestin' the wrong people. That's good enough fer me. Besides, Blimpey's gettin' a bit restless. It'll do 'im good to get back to work."

Smythe gaped at her, but as she'd already started for the door, she didn't notice. He took off after her. He wondered what on earth they were going to do now. Blast a Spaniard, he thought, did everyone in bloomin' London know about their investigating?

Betsy was furious. She snatched up the bowl of mashed potatoes and whirled about toward the sink.

"Uh, Smythe's not 'ad supper yet," Wiggins reminded her, "and I know 'e's right fond of Mrs. Goodge's potatoes."

"Then he ought to have been here in time for supper," Betsy said tartly. She put the bowl on the counter and hurried back to the table. Supper was over and done with. Mrs. Jeffries had already gone upstairs to meet the inspector at the front door and Mrs. Goodge had gone to her room, so it was just her and Wiggins left to clear up.

Wiggins sensed that perhaps he ought to tread lightly. Betsy didn't look very happy. She'd been all right when they first sat down to have their meal; but as it got later and later and the coachman hadn't come home, the maid had gotten quieter and quieter.

"I'm going to clear up," she said, "and if he comes home hungry, that's just too bad." She began snatching up the half-empty bowls and the dirty plates.

Wiggins opened his mouth to protest just as Mrs. Goodge came back into the kitchen. He looked at her for help, but she simply gave her head a barely imperceptible shake. He clamped his mouth shut. Maybe it would be best if he stayed out of this, Smythe wouldn't starve if he missed his supper.

Upstairs, they heard the front door open. Mrs. Goodge, who wanted to distract the maid out of her worry and temper, said, "I expect that's the inspector. You go up and see, then pop back down and I'll fix him a tray."

"But I wanted to finish clearing up," Betsy protested. "He usually has a sherry first."

In the old days, Mrs. Goodge would have flailed the girl with the back side of her tongue for daring to question an instruction, but not now. Betsy was too much like family to be treated like that. But nonetheless, she wanted the girl to have a moment to cool down just in case Smythe came home.

"I know," Mrs. Goodge said firmly. "But sometimes the inspector wants to eat right away, especially if he's planning on going back out."

Betsy put the dirty dishes down on the counter by the sink. "All right, I'll nip up and see what's what."

Wiggins waited till he heard her footsteps on the back stairs, then he said, "I think she's a bit annoyed with Smythe. He didn't tell 'er where 'e was goin' tonight."

"He's done that lots of times," Mrs. Goodge said as she stacked the dirty dishes in a neat pile. "I don't know why she's getting in such a state about it this evening."

"Since they got engaged, they've got an agreement," Wiggins told the cook. "I 'eard 'em talkin' about it. Neither of 'em is to go off without lettin' the other know where they're goin'."

"You heard them discussing this?" Mrs. Goodge fixed the footman with a hard stare. "In front of you?"

Wiggins had the good grace to blush. "Well, uh, they didn't really talk about it in front of me."

"You were eavesdropping?"

"It weren't my fault," he argued. "I was waitin' by the back door for Fred one night, and the two of 'em was in 'ere natterin' away. They didn't bother to keep their voices down. What could I do? I didn't want 'em to know I'd been there all along, so Fred and me waited till they went upstairs before we come in."

Mrs. Goodge sighed. "It's all right, Wiggins. Mind you, the next time you find yourself in that situation, you might call out so they'll know you're there."

He grinned. "But that'd spoil all the fun now, wouldn't it?"

Upstairs, Mrs. Jeffries met the inspector as he came in the front door. "Good evening, sir."

"Good evening." He handed her his bowler. "How is the household?"

"We're all well, Inspector. How was your day?" She helped him off with his coat.

"It was very difficult," he said with a sigh. "Very difficult indeed."

"Would you care to relax with a sherry, sir?"

"Actually"—he gave her a weary smile—"I believe I'll just have my dinner. I shall retire early tonight, Mrs. Jeffries. I'm very tired."

Mrs. Jeffries smiled serenely. "Of course, sir. I'll bring your tray to the dining room."

She met Betsy by the back stairs. "Can you bring up the inspector's tray, please?"

Betsy's eyes widened. "You mean he's not having a sherry?"

"Not tonight; he seems very tired," the housekeeper replied. "I doubt I shall get much out of him tonight."

Betsy turned on her heel. "I'll bring it right up."

Mrs. Jeffries went back to the dining room. If she was lucky, she might get a bit of information out of him before he ate.

The kitchen at Upper Edmonton Gardens was quiet as the grave when Smythe came in at half past ten. "Betsy," he whispered as he poked his head around the door, "did you wait up for me?"

But the room was empty as well as silent. "Blast," he muttered. "She's not 'ere."

"I expect she's a bit annoyed with you."

Smythe jumped and whirled about. "Cor blimey, Mrs. Jeffries, you did startle me some. Uh, you think Betsy's a bit put out?"

Mrs. Jeffries held a covered tray in her hand. "Oh, I

think it's a bit more serious than being 'put out,' as you call it." She went toward the table. "But I expect you're hungry. I saved you a bite of supper."

"Thanks, Mrs. Jeffries, I'm right famished." He followed her to the table and slid into his seat.

"Smythe, I'm not one to interfere." She put a plate of cold roast beef, cheese, pickled onions and bread in front of him. "But I do believe your relationship with Betsy might be a bit smoother if you didn't disappear before meals."

He flipped his serviette onto his lap and picked up his fork. "I'm sorry, Mrs. Jeffries, I ought to 'ave told both you and Betsy where I was off to, but I honestly thought I'd be back before supper was over. I only meant to go across town and give someone a message. But things got complicated and instead of giving the message, I got drug off to see the person in the flesh . . . and it was one of them situations where you're not sure what you ought to do and you don't want to make trouble because you really need some 'elp." He paused for a breath. "Am I makin' any sense at all?"

"I think so." She smiled kindly. "I take it you were in a situation where you had no choice but to carry on once you'd arrived at your destination."

He nodded eagerly and stuffed a bite of cheese into his mouth. "That's right. One of my sources 'asn't been around lately, and I needed to get a message to 'im. Only instead of takin' my message, I got took to see 'im in the flesh."

Mrs. Jeffries sat down across from him. "Were you successful in your inquiries?"

"That I was, Mrs. Jeffries." He grinned, thinking of how annoyed Blimpey was when Lila escorted him into the small, rather nice cottage by the river where he was holed up. Blimpey hadn't been at his usual haunts for a very good reason. His gout had flared up badly. "I went to see a feller by the name of Blimpey Groggins."

"And was he able to help you?"

Smythe glanced up as footsteps pounded down the back stairs.

"I thought I 'eard you," Wiggins said cheerfully. He ambled toward the table and plopped down next to the coachman. "Where ya been? I think Betsy's a bit miffed at ya. She kept starin' at your empty place at supper."

Mrs. Jeffries turned her head slightly, as another, lighter pair of feet came down the back stairs. "Smythe was held up by something rather important," she said loudly.

Startled by the housekeeper's tone, Wiggins jerked in his chair. "Cor blimey, Mrs. Jeffries, you give me a fright there."

Betsy came into the kitchen. She'd taken off her apron and had a soft lavender wool shawl around her shoulders. "So you finally came home." She looked disapprovingly at Smythe. "It's about time. I was worried."

Smythe smiled in relief. She looked annoyed, but not angry enough to tear a strip off him. "I'm sorry, I should 'ave told ya where I was off to, but I thought I'd be 'ome in time for supper. Then, once I got there, things sort of got out of 'and."

"Got where?" Betsy crossed her arms over her chest.

"The Artichoke Tavern." He took another quick bite of food. "It's down by the docks. I wanted to get a message to one of my sources . . . but once I got there, I got drug off to see 'im and I didn't want to upset anyone as this source is bloomin' good, if you know what I mean and . . ."

"Did you find out anything?" Betsy interrupted. She slipped into the chair next to him.

Taken aback, he blinked. For a brief moment he was a bit put out that she wasn't more interested in where he'd been. Then he got a hold of himself and thanked his lucky stars that the lass trusted him. "I found out plenty. Now I know why Harrison Nye's name sounded so familiar to me; there was a lot of talk about the bloke when 'e first come to London."

"What kind of talk?" Wiggins asked.

"Let me tell it my own way, lad," Smythe said, "otherwise it'll not make much sense. "No one really knows much about Harrison Nye's background, but what they do know is that 'e showed up one day at the offices of Mayhew and Lundt, Stockbrokers, and bought a fistful of the best stock goin'."

"What's so odd about that?" Mrs. Jeffries asked curiously. "I believe huge numbers of shares change hands each day."

"True, but I'll lay you odds the people doin' the tradin' aren't handin' over gold to buy 'em with. That's what Nye did. He paid for his stock in gold. That's 'ow come I knew 'is name. It were the talk of London."

Mrs. Jeffries was fairly certain that the only people who had heard about Harrison Nye were those who had a genuine interest in the City's financial community. Smythe, even all those years ago, was such a person. Smythe was a rich man. He'd made a fortune in Australia and then come back to England and invested his money. He'd worked for the inspector's Aunt Euphemia. When she'd left this house and a sizable fortune to Gerald Witherspoon, Euphemia had made Smythe promise to 'hang about and keep an eye on the boy' for a few months. But once Betsy had arrived and they'd started their investigating, it had become impossible for him to leave. He enjoyed himself far too much to want to go anywhere else. However, as the coachman went to great pains to keep his true financial worth a secret from the rest of the household (except Betsy), she could hardly blurt this observation out for all and sundry to hear. "I'm sure it was."

Wiggins scratched his chin. "You mean this bloke just slapped a bunch of gold bars or nuggets down onto the counter to buy 'is shares?"

"Just about," Smythe replied. "Supposedly, he did 'is dealin' first, decidin' what 'e wanted to buy and such, then 'e walked over to the bank and exchanged his nuggets for cash. That set a few tongues waggin', I can tell ya."

"Where did he get the gold?" Betsy asked.

"My source wasn't rightly sure."

"Maybe 'e stole it?" Wiggins suggested eagerly.

"Not likely." Smythe shook his head. "My source would 'ave known if there'd been a theft of that much gold in the past twenty years. We're not talkin' about a few nuggets 'ere."

"Nye probably didn't get it in England," Mrs. Jeffries said thoughtfully. "It's hardly a common medium of exchange. So that means Nye probably procured the nuggets somewhere overseas."

"That's what my source thought," Smythe agreed. "I'm goin' to be seein' 'im again tomorrow, 'e ought to know more by then. 'E's workin' on it." He clamped his mouth shut as he realized what he'd just revealed. Blast a Spaniard, no one was supposed to know that his "sources" were anything but ordinary people who just happened to have information about the victim. He glanced quickly around the table and to his amazement, realized that none of them appeared to understand the implied logic behind his statement. Then again, it was late and they were tired. Tomorrow was another day, though, and they all had good memories. "Uh, 'e's right curious about Nye 'imself," he sputtered quickly, "and when I started askin' questions, he said he knew someone who might know where Nye got the gold. I thought I'd drop around and see if 'e found anything useful out, but then again, I might not."

"I think you ought to find out as much as you can about the gold," Mrs. Jeffries said. "Old sins cast long shadows."

"What's that got to do with anythin'?" Wiggins asked.

"Nothing, probably." She shrugged. "But it popped into my head as Smythe was speaking and I've learned that sometimes it pays to take heed of what comes out of your mouth."

And sometimes it pays to keep your mouth shut, Smythe thought. He hoped the others believed his lame excuse about his source being "curious." It would be right embarrassin' to ever 'ave to admit that his source was a professional and that Smythe had been buying information about their cases for years.

Mrs. Jeffries was waiting in the dining room when the inspector came down for his breakfast. She was determined to find out everything he'd learned the day before, and she was also determined to pass what they'd found out to him. They really must get cracking on this case; otherwise, someone was going to get away with murder.

"Good morning, sir," she said cheerfully as Witherspoon came into the room. "I do hope you slept well. You looked dreadfully tired last night."

"I slept very well, thank you." He pulled out his chair, sat down and gazed happily at the food on the table. "This smells wonderful. I warn you, Mrs. Jeffries, you might have to dash down to the kitchen for seconds. I'm very hungry this morning."

"Eat hardy, sir. I expect you need to keep your strength up, what with this dreadful case." Mrs. Jeffries placed a cup of hot tea she'd just poured by his plate. "I honestly don't see how you do it."

He took a piece of toast from the rack. "Oh, it's not that difficult. Mind you, yesterday did seem a bit long, but then again, we were rather busy." He told her about his visit to Mrs. Nye. She listened carefully, taking in all the details and storing them carefully in her mind. She had dozens of questions she wanted to ask, but she had the feeling this wasn't the time.

"And then I had the most extraordinary interview with Oscar Daggett's physician." He took a quick sip from his cup and a bite of toast.

"His physician?" Mrs. Jeffries prompted. Sometimes the inspector could get a tad distracted by food. "I take it you learned something important."

Witherspoon scooped a forkful of scrambled egg off his plate. "I think so. But I'm not quite sure what to make of it." He popped the food into his mouth and chewed, his expression thoughtful.

Mrs. Jeffries hid her impatience behind a smile. "Really, sir?"

"Oh yes, it's all quite strange." He told her everything he'd learned from Dr. Wiltshire. "So you see, I don't really know if Daggett's thinking he was going to die had anything to do with his visit to Nye or not. It's a bit of a puzzle, but I do tend to think there must be a connection of some sort or another."

"Yes, sir, I think I understand what you mean." She sat down in her usual place. "After all, Dagget had been in his bed, ill and waiting to die until just after the doctor told him there was nothing wrong with him. Then he leaps up and tears out into the night. If the doctor's recollection of the timing of these events is correct, that's the only place Daggett could have gone . . ." She hoped he was getting the drift of her thinking.

"I most certainly do," he interrupted. "After all, Nelda Smith was sent out to post a letter."

Mrs. Jeffries stared at him. She didn't quite see what he was getting at, but she'd learned in the past that it was always important to listen. The inspector could make connections that she sometimes missed. "I don't quite see how . . ."

"I'm not sure myself," he agreed, "but it seems to me that perhaps there was some connection between that letter and the visit to Harrison Nye."

Betsy stuck her head in the dining room. "Excuse me, sir, but Constable Barnes is coming up the front stairs. Should I bring him in?"

"Of course," Witherspoon replied. "Mrs. Jeffries, do bring another cup. I'm sure the constable will want some tea."

A moment later, they heard the front door open and Betsy ushered Constable Barnes into the dining room.

"Good morning, sir, Mrs. Jeffries." Barnes smiled with genuine pleasure at the housekeeper. "Sorry to interrupt your breakfast, sir, but I've had some news, and I thought you'd like it as soon as possible."

"That's quite all right, Constable, do sit down and have a cup of tea." He gestured toward an empty chair. "Then you can give me a full report."

"Would you care for some breakfast, Constable?" Mrs. Jeffries asked as she poured another cup of Darjeeling.

"I've had breakfast, thank you." He nodded his thanks as he took the cup. "We've heard back from the Lancashire Constabulary, and I thought you'd want to know right away."

Now that the constable was here, Mrs. Jeffries could hardly continue questioning the inspector. Reluctantly, she got to her feet and busied herself brushing at the nonexistent crumbs on the tablecloth. She was hoping the constable would get on with it so she could hear what he had to say before good manners actually forced her from the room. Of course, she would nip back and eavesdrop, but it was so easy to miss something that way.

"Do sit down, Mrs. Jeffries," Witherspoon said absently. "You haven't finished your tea."

"Why thank you, sir, if you're sure I'm not interrupting." But she quickly took her seat. "I am so very curious about your cases."

Barnes smiled at her over the rim of his cup. His eyes were twinkling, and she had the distinct impression he knew precisely what she was up to. But she put that thought aside; if he did, he would keep it to himself. She hoped.

"All right, Constable, what have we heard from Lancashire?" The inspector took a bite of bacon.

"The news isn't good, Inspector. Nelda Smith didn't run off home. Her family hasn't heard a word from her."

CHAPTER 8

⸻◦⸺⸺

"I thought you'd gone for good," the boy said cheerfully. "When I turned around and saw you standin' on the corner, I was so surprised you coulda knocked me flat with mam's duster."

Smythe shifted his weight uneasily against the hard surface of the café chair. He felt guilty. He'd told this lad he'd buy him a bun and a cuppa, but that had been three days ago. Mind you, Harold was a nice lad, he hadn't held a grudge when Smythe had "accidentally" run into him again this morning. "I didn't mean to disappear. But somethin' important come up."

"Somethin' with the murder?" Harold asked eagerly.

Smythe winced inwardly, but managed to keep his expression straight. "Yeah. Like I told ya before, I work for a detective."

"I remember." Harold stuffed another bite of bun in his mouth.

"And I'd like to ask a question or two if you don't mind," Smythe finished.

"Go ahead," Harold replied. "Mam says we ought to

keep ourselves to ourselves. But I think we ought to tell what we know."

"That's right good of you, lad." Smythe tried to think of what to say. All the questions he would have asked on the day of the murder had already been answered. "Uh, do you 'appen to remember if you saw anyone near Miss Geddy's house on the night of the murder?"

Harold looked down at the table. "Well, Mam says I should keep quiet about it, because it don't mean nuthin' and if I said anything, the police might think I 'ad something to do with the killin'. She's scared of the police, she is. But I don't think that's likely."

"Why would you 'ave 'ad a reason to murder anyone?" Smythe asked casually. He knew the next few seconds would determine whether or not he got anything out of the boy. Harold was a cheerful, eager lad, but Smythe knew he was more interested in the tea and the bun than in answering questions for a stranger. Working people were deeply mistrustful of the police, often for good reason. There were a lot of coppers about that wouldn't look farther than the tip of their noses when a crime was committed, and it was usually those at the bottom of the heap that was looked at first.

"That's what I told Mam," Harold said, "but she said that since the coppers never caught that Ripper feller, they'd grab anyone they could when there was a killin'. But I don't believe that. Besides, that man were murdered hours after I was asleep."

"So you'll tell me what ya saw?"

Harold grinned. "Course I will, not that I think it's got anything to do with the killin', I don't. It were a girl, you see. When I tried to tell Mam, she said it were probably some friend of Miss Geddy's, and I was to think no more about it, but Miss Geddy didn't have friends . . ."

"Slow down, lad." Smythe held up his hand. "You're goin' too fast for me to take it all in. What girl are you talkin' about?"

Harold took a deep breath. "The girl I saw on the night

that bloke was killed. I saw her comin' down the street and then she turned into Miss Geddy's place and walked up the front door as big as you please."

"What did she do when she got to the door?"

"She pushed a letter through the mailbox on the front door, then she left. I saw her clear as day, you see. I almost spoke to her, but she seemed to be in a bit of a hurry."

"How could you tell that?" Smythe asked.

"The way she was walkin'," Harold said. "She were movin' really fast, you could tell by the way she watched all the house numbers as she walked past 'em. But that didn't seem to slow her down; once she spotted the one she wanted, she practically ran toward it."

Smythe wasn't sure what to make of this. "Did anyone else 'appen to see the woman?"

Harold's eyes narrowed suspiciously. "Don't ya believe me?"

"Course I do, boy, but it's awful easy to mistake one night for another. Are you sure it was the night of the murder that you saw this girl? You sure it wasn't the night before?"

"I'm sure," Harold said. "I know because it was that night that Mam sent me down to pub for a dram of whiskey for Da's cold. I was on my way back when I saw her. You can ask 'em down at pub, they'll tell ya I was in that night."

Smythe raised his hand. "I believe you, it's just I've got to make sure there wasn't a mix-up. What did this girl look like?"

"Well"—Harold hesitated a moment—"she was wearin' a hat and a dark coat. But she had dark hair, I could see that, she had it tucked up under a hat."

"How old do you think she might be?" Smythe was fairly sure the lad wouldn't have a clue about a woman's age, but he had to ask.

"She looked to be about sixteen or seventeen," Harold said firmly. "About the same age as my cousin Agnes.

She didn't have any wrinkles or spots, and I noticed something else, too. She had on a maid's dress. Her coat came open when she started running up the street to her fellow."

"Fellow?" Smythe leaned forward, trying to curb his excitement. "Someone was waitin' for her? Are you sure about that?"

"Sure as I'm sittin' here talkin' to you." Harold gave him a cocky grin. "He was standing on the corner. They went off together. He took her arm and everythin'." He popped the last bite of food into his mouth. "Do you think I ought to tell the police?"

Smythe wasn't sure how to answer that question. It was probably information the police ought to know, but he had to be careful. If he sent Harold along to have a chat with the police, the lad might accidentally mention that someone named Smythe had been along asking questions about the murder. "I'm not sure. That letter or whatever the girl shoved in Miss Geddy's letterbox might be important. It might 'ave somethin' to do with the murder. But then again, it might not."

Harold shrugged. "I'll keep my mouth shut, then. If it's got something to do with the murder, Miss Geddy can take it along to the police herself. She's comin' back in a few days."

Inspector Witherspoon stepped down from the hansom and onto the cobblestone road. The neighborhood where the Windemere brothers now lived was grim. On one side of the street was a factory belching soot into the sky, giving the air a faintly copper smell. In the courtyard of the factory, workers loaded barrels onto a rickety-looking wagon.

"Not the nicest area, is it, sir?" Constable Barnes said. He was staring at the row of tiny houses opposite the factory. They were all a dull, uniform gray, had no front gardens and were in various stages of disrepair. The men they wanted to interview lived in one of them. "But then people can't help being poor, can they?"

"No, it's sad that anyone has to live in such places," Witherspoon replied. He sighed inwardly. He'd grown up in a neighborhood not much better than this one, but his home had been well tended and clean. There hadn't been trash in the streets, gutters stuffed with leaves and a noisy factory fouling the air with grime. He reminded himself to count his blessings. He'd also inherited a fortune. Most people weren't so lucky. "But then again, who are we to judge? Home is home." He started off down the street. "Let's hope we can learn something from these gentlemen. I don't mind admitting it, Constable, this case isn't going very well."

"You'll sort it out, sir," Barnes said easily. "You always do."

"Gracious, I do hope so. But it doesn't look good. We've searched the whole area and we still haven't found the murder weapon . . ."

"We probably won't, sir," Barnes interrupted gently. "Dr. Bosworth agrees with Dr. Boyer's opinion. He also thinks that from the size and shape of the entry wound, the killer probably used a common old butcher knife." Barnes had "unofficially" asked their good friend, Dr. Bosworth, to have a look at the body after the police surgeon had finished the postmortem. It wasn't that he didn't think Dr. Boyer was competent; he was. But Bosworth had spent a year practicing medicine in San Francisco. Apparently they had quite a lot of murder there and, consequently, he'd become somewhat of an expert on determining what kind of wound was made with a particular kind of weapon. He'd helped them on a number of their cases, and the doctor had invariably been right in his assessments.

"I know." The inspector sighed. "Which means it's probably sitting in someone's kitchen drawer, and we'll never find it."

"You've solved lots of cases without a murder weapon," Barnes pointed out.

"*We've* solved lots of cases," Witherspoon corrected. "I

certainly didn't do it alone. You and everyone else on the force did as much as I did." He held up his hand as Barnes started to protest. "Everyone does their fair share, Constable. I couldn't solve anything without the information you and the other constables come up with. Mind you, this time, we haven't had much useful information at all. Even the house-to-house interviews haven't yielded much. No one saw or heard anything except for a few mysterious footsteps."

"It doesn't seem to make much sense, does it, sir?" Barnes commented. "But we've not spoken to everyone as yet. Something will turn up. It always does." He pointed to the house at the end of the row. "There's the house, sir. Let's hope they're home and that this isn't a wasted trip."

Barnes raised his fist to knock. But before he could strike the blow, the door flew open and a tall, thin-faced man stared out at them. "I've been expecting you," he said. "I'm John Windemere." He pulled the door open and stepped backward. "Come inside, please."

They went into a cramped hallway. A coat rack loaded with jackets, caps, coats and scarves was just inside the door. Next to it stood a tall mottled brass vase with umbrellas sticking out the top. The walls were papered in faded yellow-and-gold stripes, and there was a threadbare brown carpet runner on the floor.

John Windemere closed the door and pushed past the two policemen. "Let's go into the parlor," he said gruffly.

They followed him into a room as dismal as the hall. The furniture was as old and threadbare as the carpet. Limp white-lace curtains, now turned gray, covered two dirty windows and a fine layer of dust covered the wood surfaces of the end tables and the one lone bookcase on the far wall.

Windemere flopped down on the settee. "I suppose you want to know where my brother and I were on the night that Harrison Nye was murdered," he said.

Witherspoon and Barnes exchanged looks. It was rare

to find someone who got right to the point, so to speak. Then the inspector said, "That would be very helpful information, sir."

"You can't pin this on either of us. We've the best alibi one can have." Windemere smiled thinly. "We were at the Marylebone Police Station."

Barnes whipped out his notebook. "Were you under arrest?"

Windemere gave a short, harsh bark of a laugh. "Why else would one spend the night in such a place. Of course we were under arrest. But it wasn't our fault. We were attacked. Then the police had the sheer, unmitigated gall to arrest my brother and I instead of the real culprits."

Witherspoon frowned. "Could you give us a few more details, sir? Were you attacked by ruffians?" He didn't think that was the case; if it had been, it would have been the ruffians who'd been arrested, not the Windemere brothers.

"Ruffians. I should say so, but because they were dressed nicely and spoke with the proper accent, the police took their version of what happened as the truth."

"Why don't you tell us your version, sir?" Barnes suggested calmly. "And where is your brother, sir? Is he about?"

"My brother is at work, Constable," Windemere replied. "He clerks for a legal firm in Earls Court. He'll not be home till six."

Witherspoon's lower back began to throb. "May we sit down, Mr. Windemere? It appears as if you've quite a bit to tell us."

Wiggins smiled at the housemaid carrying the wicker basket and knew he'd struck gold. "Hortense is a nice name," he said. "It fits you very nicely. Would you like me to carry your basket?"

Hortense, who'd been walking a mile a minute since Wiggins had "accidentally" run into her coming out of the Daggett house, considered his offer. "Well, it is getting heavy, and it's quite a long ways to go yet. Here." She thrust the basket into his waiting hands. "Thanks ever so much."

He was surprised by how heavy it was. The top was covered with a white tea towel. "What's in 'ere?"

She made a face, reached over and flipped the tea towel back. A large, brown bottle was nestled snugly in a cradle of packed towels.

"What's that?" Wiggins asked in surprise. "An empty bottle?"

"That's right," Hortense replied, "I've got to drag this great, heavy thing all the way to Cromwell Road. Can you believe the foolishness of some people? Mr. Daggett, that's who I work for, he's one of those people who think they're on death's door all the time. He thinks this tonic keeps him healthy. It's nothing more than whiskey mixed with a few herbs, but he swears by the stuff. Some old woman makes it up for him, and, wouldn't you know, he ran out of it this morning. I don't usually have to go get it, but what with Nelda and her new husband showing up and havin' words with Mrs. Benchley, things got all mixed up. Instead of the footman goin' to get His Lordship's ruddy potion, I got stuck doin' it. It's not fair. That old woman lives a good mile away, and once this stupid bottle is full, it'll be even heavier comin' back. If I didn't need this position so badly, I'd do just what Nelda did and run off without a word to anyone. Mind you, I don't have a young man to marry now, do I?"

Wiggins wasn't sure how to proceed. On the one hand, he knew this girl was a mine of information, on the other hand, she looked to be a bit annoyed. Females, he'd observed, could be unpredictable when they were angry. He wanted her to talk to him, not box his ears. But there was too much at stake to back off. He had to know what had happened. He decided to proceed with caution.

"I bet you could have someone if you wanted," he said softly. He hoped he was saying the right thing. "I'm not tryin' to be forward, miss, but you're awfully pretty." It isn't exactly a lie, he thought. She's not really ugly. If she smiled a bit and put on some weight, she'd be quite nice-looking.

She stopped dead in her tracks and stared at him. Wiggins's heart sank. This girl had looked in a mirror recently.

"Do you mean that?" she asked.

Wiggins nodded. "Course I do."

A slow smile crept over her face, and she did, indeed, become prettier. "That's awfully kind of you. Where did you say you worked?" She took his arm and they started walking.

"Uh, I didn't. But I work near Holland Park, I'm a footman of sorts."

"That's nice. Is today your day out?" She smiled coyly and batted her eyelashes.

Wiggins had the feeling he might end up regretting this morning's snooping. Hortense might be a very nice girl, but he wasn't really interested in her, only in what she had to tell him about the Daggett household. "Uh, yeah. Actually, I don't get much time away from my work. But sometimes I go out on Saturdays . . ." It was a safe bet that a housemaid wouldn't get a Saturday afternoon off from her duties. They almost always got a day off in the middle of the week and Sunday mornings for church.

"That's too bad," she continued. "My afternoon out is Wednesday. Mind you, now that Nelda's gone for sure, I might be able to get Saturday afternoon off as well. That would be nice, wouldn't it?"

"Uh, yeah, it sure would. Who's Nelda?"

Betsy smiled at the girl sitting next to her on the park bench. "Now don't worry, I'm sure that you'll still have your position. Mrs. Nye isn't going to sell the house right away, is she?"

Arlene Hill, a tiny woman with a narrow face, dark brown eyes and olive complexion, shrugged her thin shoulders. "Who knows what she'll do? Now that he's gone, she's her own mistress, isn't she?"

Betsy, who hadn't had much luck at all on this case, had finally done something right. She'd gone to the Nye house just to have a look at it, get the lay of the land, so to speak, and she'd seen this girl coming out of the side servants' entrance. She'd followed her, of course, and then struck up a conversation with her when she'd been gazing in a shop window. As it turned out this was Arlene Hill's afternoon out and she had no one to spend her few free hours with. Betsy had told her it was her day out as well and suggested they take a walk around Hyde Park. It hadn't taken Betsy long to get the conversation around to the recent murder of Arlene's late master. Arlene was a bit shy at first, but under Betsy's easy approach, she soon had the girl talking freely. As a matter of fact, by the time they had reached the park bench, the girl was talking a blue streak. Arlene was lonely. She didn't have a lot of close friends in the household. Nye's rule about the servants gossiping about the master and mistress apparently had the effect of virtually shutting people up altogether.

"Most women don't like to leave their homes," Betsy said conversationally. "But mind you, you never know what people will do when they're grief-stricken."

Arlene laughed. "Grief-stricken? Her? Not bloomin' likely."

Betsy pretended to be shocked. "Oh dear, the master and mistress didn't get along? That does make it hard sometimes. Especially for those of us who have to work for them."

"They got on all right," she replied, "but now that he's dead, she can do what she likes. She couldn't when she was married to him, could she?"

"Why not? I thought you said the family was rich."

"He had plenty," Arlene replied. "But she hadn't a farthing. Oh, she's from a toff-nosed family, that's for sure, just like her cousin. But they're both poor as church mice.

Mr. Nye was the one with the money, wasn't he? Now it's all hers. I know that for a fact because I overheard her tellin' Mr. Bancroft how they'd never have to worry again, how he'd left it all to her."

"Was Mr. Nye a mean husband, then?" Betsy asked.

Arlene looked thoughtful. "He wasn't mean, but you could tell he kept a tight fist on the purse."

Betsy snorted. "That sounds like most men."

"But not all of 'em are like that." Arlene laughed. "The last family I worked for, the missus spent like a drunken sailor and her husband never said a word about it. Mr. Nye would pay the bills, but he always made her squirm a bit, asked her questions about each and every thing she'd bought. You could tell she didn't like it. She was always in a bad mood after she'd been into his study at the end of the month." Arlene laughed again. "But I've got no reason to complain. Come the end of this month, she'll not be answerin' to him anymore, at least that's what I heard her tellin' Mr. Bancroft."

Betsy wanted to steer the conversation along to the night of the murder. "It must be frightening, living in a house where the master's been stabbed to death."

"Oh no, it's exciting. Now that he's dead, we can talk about him all we like," Arlene said. "It's not like before. Like I told you when we were walking over here, we had to be real careful what we said around that house, even to each other. He was a bit of an old preacher about us gossipin'. Mind you, we do have to be careful. It wasn't just Mr. Nye that didn't want us talkin'; she's almost as bad as he was."

Betsy tried to think of what else to ask. She wasn't surprised by the Nyes' rule of silence. It was probably the sort of silly rule most rich houses would have if they thought they had a chance of making it work properly. She was rather amazed at how well it had apparently worked at the Nye house. But now wasn't the time to discuss that. "I guess you're right. As long as you knew the killer isn't in the house with you, it would be exciting."

"I was a bit disappointed that that nice-looking Constable Griffiths didn't want to ask me a few questions." Arlene sighed. "He's got ever such nice ginger-colored hair."

"He didn't speak to you?"

"No."

"So you didn't talk to a policeman at all?" Betsy pressed. She was sure that couldn't be right. Inspector Witherspoon was very conscientious. He would expect everyone in the victim's household to be interviewed, especially the servants.

"Oh I spoke to Constable Griffiths, but only for half a second. He got called away to take care of something, then Mr. Duffy sent me upstairs to air out the top bedrooms. By the time I got back downstairs, the police had gone." Arlene smiled slyly. "Too bad for him, that's what I say. There's plenty I could have told the police about that night."

The afternoon was getting old by the time Witherspoon and Barnes were finished verifying the Windemere brothers' alibi at the Marylebone Police Station. They came out onto the busy high street. A cold breeze had swept in from the north and the air was heavy with the feel of rain. The inspector looked up at the gathering clouds. "It's almost teatime, Constable. Let's go back to Upper Edmonton Gardens and have a cuppa. What do you say? It'll be better than anything we can get in a tea shop or a café. We can pick up some umbrellas as well. I think we're going to need them before the day is out."

Barnes's craggy face split into a grin. "You'll not have to ask me twice, sir. Do you think Mrs. Goodge has made scones?"

"I do hope so." Witherspoon waved at a passing hansom. "There's quite a good chance of it, you know. She always seems to bake a lot when I'm on a murder case."

The cab pulled up to the curb and they climbed inside.

"Number twenty-two Upper Edmonton Gardens," Witherspoon called to the driver. "It's going to be a very long day for us," he said as he leaned back against the seat. "We've got to review the rest of those house-to-house reports, and I think it might be a good idea to have another interview with Oscar Daggett."

"Yes, sir, I agree. So far, he's about the only suspect we've got. It's too bad both the Windemere brothers were in custody. They'd have made good suspects. They certainly had reason to hate Nye."

By the time the hansom reached Upper Edmonton Gardens, it had started to sprinkle. They paid off the cab and hurried inside. "Hello," the inspector called as he took off his hat and coat.

"Good afternoon, sir," Mrs. Jeffries said from the top of the back stairs. She sounded out of breath. "How lovely to have you home. Constable Barnes, how nice to see you again."

Witherspoon beamed at his housekeeper. "We weren't far away, and I was hoping we might be in time for tea." He sniffed the air. "I say, is that scones I smell?"

Mrs. Jeffries kept her expression calm and mentally crossed her fingers, hoping the inspector wouldn't ask where everyone was this afternoon. She could hardly admit they were all out snooping. As the household was going to have a meeting this afternoon, they were all due back shortly, but they certainly weren't here now. Furthermore, Mrs. Goodge had had her sources coming through her kitchen all day, and the supply of scones was dwindling fast. She had someone in the kitchen right at this very moment. "I believe it is, sir. If you and the constable will have a seat in the drawing room, I'll bring up a tray."

"Oh, that won't be necessary, you mustn't go to any trouble." He started for the back stairs. "We'll have our tea in the kitchen. Much cheerier there than up here. Come along, Constable, let's get some of Mrs. Goodge's delicious scones."

"It's no trouble, sir." Mrs. Jeffries trailed behind the two men.

"No, no, I quite like the kitchen," Witherspoon called over his shoulder. "Is Fred about?"

"He's in the back garden," Mrs. Jeffries replied as she clambered down the stairs behind the men.

But the cook had matters well in hand. In the few minutes between their realization that the inspector had come home and his actual arrival in the kitchen, Mrs. Goodge had managed everything. She'd gotten rid of her source, dumped the dirty dishes in the sink, thrown a clean tea towel over the plate of scones and put the jam and butter back into the larder. "Good afternoon, sir. Constable Barnes." Mrs. Goodge gave them her best smile and brushed her hands off on her apron. "Have you come home for tea, then?"

"Indeed we have." Witherspoon took his place at the head of the table and waved Constable Barnes into the chair next to him. "Your scones are simply too irresistible."

"I'll make the tea," Mrs. Jeffries murmured.

"Not to worry, I've put the kettle on," the cook called cheerfully. She started for the dry larder in the hall. "It should only take a moment."

"Where is everyone?" Witherspoon asked.

Mrs. Jeffries grabbed the teapot off the shelf. "I sent Betsy to the greengrocer's up on Holland Park Road, and Smythe's at Howard's—" She broke off, not wanting to say too much in case someone showed up while the inspector was still here.

"And I sent Wiggins off to get me my rheumatism medicine," Mrs. Goodge said as she came back into the room. She was carrying the jam jar and the butter dish. She put them down on the table and whipped the tea towel off the top of the scones. "Do help yourselves," she offered. "Now, how is your case going, sir?"

Within a few minutes, they were having tea and talking about the murder of Harrison Nye as though they did it every afternoon. By the time the inspector and Barnes were leaving, they'd gotten every detail of the day's activities out of the two men.

Mrs. Jeffries breathed a sigh of relief as she closed the door behind them. She dashed back to the kitchen. "That was a close one," she said to the cook.

Mrs. Goodge nodded. "It certainly was, but it was worth it. We found out an awful lot of information. When the others get here, let's not let them muck about. We've a lot to get through today."

She was true to her word as well. When the others arrived she hustled them to the table, got the tea poured and the buns distributed in mere seconds. "Now," she said, "if no one objects, I'd like to go first."

No one had the nerve to say a word. Sometimes, it was best to let the cook have her way.

"Good, first of all, I found out that my old friend Jane was wrong, someone was dismissed from the Nye house."

"What'd they done?" Luty asked. "Opened their mouth when the boss was in the kitchen? Silliest thing I ever heard of, tellin' your servants they can't gossip."

"It is silly," Mrs. Goodge agreed. To her mind, gossip was one of the things that made life worth living. "But that's not why the girl was sacked and oddly enough it wasn't Harrison Nye that got rid of her, it was Mrs. Nye. The girl was accused of stealing one of Mrs. Nye's nightdresses."

"She pinched a nightgown?" Smythe asked incredulously.

"That's what she was accused of doing," Mrs. Goodge replied. "As to whether or not the girl was a thief, that's open to how you see things. The girl claims she found the nightdress under a cupboard by the back door, tucked up in the corner like. What's odd is that she wasn't sacked because they found the nightdress amongst her things, she was sacked when she took it to the butler and told him what she'd found."

Hatchet's face creased in confusion. "I'm afraid I don't quite understand."

"What I'm sayin' is that my source said the girl wouldn't have been sacked at all if she hadn't tried to do what's right. If she'd just put the nightdress back where she'd found it, she'd still have a position."

"Are you suggesting she might be the killer?" Hatchet asked cautiously. He didn't wish to offend the cook. He had a great respect for her abilities to ferret out information. But stabbing one's employer because one had been sacked seemed a bit extreme.

"I don't think so, this happened over a year ago, but I did think it was worth mentioning." It probably meant nothing, but one never knew what was important and what wasn't until the very end.

"Anything else, Mrs. Goodge?" Mrs. Jeffries asked.

"That's it for me," the cook replied. "I'll let you tell 'em what we heard from the inspector."

"The inspector was 'ere?" Smythe picked up his tea and took a sip.

"He and Constable Barnes stopped in late this afternoon to have tea. We found out a few interesting tidbits," she said. "We can eliminate the Windemere brothers as suspects. I know they were both at the Nye house that night, and they certainly had reason to want Nye dead, but they couldn't have done it. They were locked up in the Marylebone Police Station when Harrison Nye was stabbed."

"They were under arrest? What for?" Betsy exclaimed. She did want to hurry things on a bit, she was eager to tell everyone what she'd learned today from Arlene Hill.

"Fighting," Mrs. Jeffries replied. "Apparently when they were on their way home from the Nye house, they happened upon one of their former clients coming out of a pub. The client, who apparently was most unhappy with the kind of representation he'd once received from John Windemere, started insulting them. Both of the brothers replied in kind. Several of the client's friends then came out of the pub and joined in the shouting. That led to some shoving, which in turn led to fisticuffs. By the time the constable arrived to break it up, half the pub was involved. But it was the Windemere brothers who were carted off to jail. So I'm afraid we'll have to look elsewhere for our murderer."

"Didn't they lose their solicitin' business eleven years ago?" Wiggins asked.

"That's correct." Mrs. Jeffries took a sip from her cup.

Luty looked incredulous. "You mean someone waited eleven years to punch 'em in the nose? Nell's bells, they musta been really bad lawyers."

"Apparently so. Unfortunately, for us it means we must still keep digging on this case." Mrs. Jeffries looked around the table. "Smythe, why don't you go next."

He shot a quick glance at Betsy. He could tell by the expression on her face that she had a lot to report, and he didn't want to steal her thunder. But she gave him a smile so he knew she didn't mind. "All right, then. I went back and finally 'ad that chat with the lad that lives across the way from Frieda Geddy's house." He gave them a quick report on his meeting with Harold.

"So Nelda Smith did run off," Luty said eagerly. "Good fer her."

"But not before she shoved something through Frieda Geddy's postbox," Smythe pointed out.

"It was a letter," Wiggins said quickly. "I know because I had a talk with Hortense today. You know, the maid who works for Daggett, the one who was so worried something 'ad 'appened to her friend. Well, seems Nelda and her new husband showed up at the Daggett 'ouse today to get Nelda's trunk. Accordin' to Hortense, there was a right old dustup, and words were exchanged. Daggett was screamin' at Nelda that he wanted 'is letter back and she was shoutin' back that if 'e wanted it, 'e could 'auls 'is buns to Fulham and get it 'imself."

Luty cackled. "Did she actually say that?"

"And a bit more." Wiggins grinned. "Hortense said Daggett was so furious 'e looked like 'e was goin' to 'ave an attack of some sort. But there weren't much Daggett could do to the girl. She had her husband with 'er and 'e's a decent-sized bloke who didn't take kindly to the way Daggett talked to his new missus. The 'ousekeeper sent the footman up to get the girl's trunk, and they left, but not before the whole 'ousehold knew that on the day of the murder, Oscar Daggett sent Nelda to Fulham with a letter addressed to Frieda Geddy."

Betsy sank back in her chair. Compared to all this, what she'd learned from Arlene didn't seem to amount to much. But she would tell the others what little she knew, if this lot shut up long enough to give her a chance.

"That means there's a definite connection between Geddy and Daggett," Mrs. Jeffries said, "and it means he lied about it to the police as well. He certainly didn't tell the inspector he'd sent his maid to Dunbarton Street with a letter." Her mind was working furiously trying to sort out all the information into some kind of meaningful pattern.

"Cor blimey, this is startin' to give me a 'eadache." Wiggins laughed. "But it's a good ache, like me 'ead's so full of facts it's goin' to explode."

Smythe leaned forward eagerly. "There's somethin' else I 'aven't told you. Frieda Geddy is comin' home. She sent Mrs. Moff a telegram askin' her to accept delivery of a trunk that'll be arriving tomorrow."

Except for Mrs. Jeffries, everyone at the table started talking at once, trying to figure out just what was going on with this case.

"I know what we've got to do," the housekeeper suddenly announced.

The group fell silent, and everyone looked at her.

"We've got to get that letter. It's the key to everything."

"But it's in Miss Geddy's front hall," Mrs. Goodge pointed out. "I don't see how we can get our hands on it, short of breaking into the house."

Mrs. Jeffries smiled. "I know. But that's precisely what we'll have to do."

CHAPTER 9

"What I'm asking you to do might be difficult," Mrs. Jeffries began, "and I'll understand if you're not willing to put yourself in that kind of jeopardy."

"Don't fret, Mrs. Jeffries," Smythe said cheerfully, "it'll be fine. We can nip in and out in two shakes of a lamb's tail."

"I shall be happy to lend my assistance to the endeavor," Hatchet said as he rubbed his hands together with relish.

"You always get the fun jobs." Luty glared at her butler. She knew that no matter how much she wanted to, no one at the table would hear of her going along on this adventure. Even if she took her gun with her.

"Now, madam," Hatchet said calmly, "This is a job for the men. You know it would be far more efficient if Smythe and I—"

"And me," Wiggins protested. "I'm one of the men 'round 'ere, you know."

"Of course you are," Mrs. Jeffries assured the lad. "But before we do anything, we really must decide if it's possible to even get into the house."

"We'll get in." Smythe smiled confidently. "But I think we ought to wait until later tonight. There's workin' people in that neighborhood, so they'll be to bed early. We ought to plan on bein' at the 'ouse around eleven o'clock."

"That's a good idea," Mrs. Jeffries agreed as she rose to her feet.

"Now hold on a minute." Luty slapped her hand against the table. "Just because you all are chompin' at the bit to bust into Frieda Geddy's house—"

"I would hardly put it like that, madam," Hatchet interrupted huffily. "We're on a mission of justice to retrieve a piece of evidence that may have a direct bearing on catching a killer."

"Oh, put a sock in it, Hatchet," Luty snapped. "No matter how you try to dress it up, it's still a case of bustin' into someone's house without so much as a by-your-leave. I ain't got no quarrel with that. Hepzibah's right, we do need that letter. But you could at least see if me and Betsy has anything to add to this here meeting."

"I'm dreadfully sorry, Luty. You're absolutely right." Mrs. Jeffries sank back into her chair. "I should have made sure that everyone had their chance to speak. . . ."

Luty waved off the apology. "Not to worry, Hepzibah, I know you're all excited like and we've got a lot to do to get everything ready for tonight, but I've got somethin' to report. I found out where Harrison Nye got that gold."

For once, even Hatchet had the good grace to look embarrassed. "Very good, madam. You're right, of course. We should have waited until everyone had said their piece before we began making plans."

Luty eyed him sternly for a moment and then she grinned. "No harm done. Now, as I was sayin', I found out all about that gold and you're not goin' to believe where it came from. The Transvaal."

"Where's that?" Wiggins asked.

"South Africa," Luty continued excitedly. "But that

ain't the good part. I guess what I should have said is you'll never guess *who* it came from."

"But you're going to tell us, aren't you, madam?" Hatchet said patiently. He was quite prepared to let her have her moment in the sun.

"It came from a gold mine that was orginally owned by Oscar Daggett, Harrison Nye and Viktor Geddy, Frieda Geddy's father," Luty announced. "I found the connection. Frieda Geddy's father was in business with the other two. Fifteen years ago, Daggett and Nye bought into Geddy's claim. Geddy was a Dutchman from Holland and the original owner of the claim. But it was a bust. They'd worked it for over six months and hadn't found as much as a nugget. Then Viktor Geddy was killed in a wagon accident. Daggett and Nye, both of whom were English, bought Geddy's share from Frieda Geddy for the price of her ticket back to England. Two weeks later, they hit pay dirt."

"Cor blimey, poor Frieda Geddy," Wiggins said sympathetically. "If her father had just hung on for another fortnight, she'd been rich."

"I'm sure that's precisely what she thought as well," Mrs. Jeffries murmured. To her mind, it had become even more imperative that they get their hands on that letter.

"Anyways, I think findin' all this out is pretty important," Luty said bluntly. "Nye and Daggett worked the mine until it went dry. Nye, probably because he didn't trust banks, kept a good portion of his share of the loot in gold nuggets. Rumor has it that he brought a couple of trunk loads of 'em to England when he came back."

"I wonder if Nye and Daggett knew about the gold before they offered Frieda her passage back to England for her share?" Mrs. Jeffries muttered.

Luty shrugged. "Frieda Geddy accused them of doing just that. Nye threatened to sue her for defamation of character if she pursued the matter. Remember, the next time she saw either of them, they was rich, and she was livin' in that little house in Fulham."

"I'll bet that's how Harrison Nye's fortune started," Wiggins added eagerly. "I'll bet he used the money from the gold to do all his buyin' and sellin' . . ."

"Accordin' to my source, that's exactly how it all started. That's how come he ended up richer than Daggett. Nye put his money to work for him, Daggett just made a few business investments and then spent the rest of his time worryin' about his health." Luty pursed her lips in disgust. "Anyway, that's all I've got."

Mrs. Jeffries turned to Betsy. "Do you have anything you'd like to report?"

Betsy tried not to be depressed, but it was difficult. Everyone but her had found out something really important, something that would help solve the case. She decided to keep her little bit to herself until their next meeting. Maybe it wouldn't sound so pathetic tomorrow. "Not really. Oh, I did learn that it was Mrs. Nye who put the Windemere brothers on the guest list that night, not her husband. I spoke to one of the Nye housemaids. She saw Mrs. Nye add them to the top of the guest list after her husband had given it back to her. That's all."

Smythe gave her a quick, puzzled glance. He was sure she had something more to tell them. But from the look she shot him, he decided to keep his opinion to himself. The lass would say her piece in her own good time.

"That's odd, isn't it. I wonder why she wanted them present that night." Mrs. Jeffries tried to keep her mind on Betsy's information, but frankly, she was too excited to concentrate on anything but getting their hands on that letter. "Oh well, I'm sure we'll sort it out eventually. Now, perhaps we ought to make plans. Luty, can you and Hatchet come back tonight?"

"The madam has a previous engagement," Hatchet said quickly.

"Hogwash," Luty shot back. "I'm not goin' to waste my time at some silly dinner party . . ."

"It'll take us a good two hours to get there and get back here," Smythe pointed out. "If we leave 'ere at ten o'clock, that'd put us back at midnight. You go along in your carriage and I'll pop along to Howard's and get the inspector's for us to use tonight. Will that do ya?" Smythe didn't want an all-out war on his hands. Luty could be very stubborn. For that matter, so could Hatchet.

"I think that's a wonderful idea," Mrs. Jeffries interjected. "The inspector won't need his carriage, not in the middle of a case, and that way, you can have your driver bring you back here after your dinner party."

"Which will give me a ride home," Hatchet added.

"Well, all right," Luty muttered. "But I'll be here before eleven, you can count on that. I only accepted the invitation so I could pump a few of the other guests about our murder."

They broke up a few minutes later. Mrs. Jeffries went upstairs to do some thinking, Wiggins took Fred out for a walk, Mrs. Goodge went to the dry larder to make her grocery list and Betsy hurried up the back stairs. But she wasn't quite fast enough and Smythe caught her on the landing. He grabbed her elbow, swung her around and gave her a fast kiss.

She kissed him back and then pushed him away, but he kept a firm grip on her arms. "Someone will see us," she whispered.

"I don't care," he replied. He searched her face carefully. "Is something botherin' you?"

She wanted to stay irritated, but she couldn't. It was nice to know that he cared so much about her. "Well, not really. Oh, it's just that today everyone else had something interesting to report and all I found out from that silly Arlene was that on the night of the murder she heard footsteps on the back stairs and saw Mrs. Nye change the guest list."

"Why didn't you tell everyone about the footsteps? That could be an important clue."

"You know as well as I do that in a household that size a few footsteps aren't going to mean anything except that someone got hungry and snuck down to the kitchen for a bite of bread."

That was probably precisely what had happened, but Smythe didn't want Betsy to think her contribution wasn't important. "But you don't know that for certain . . ."

"Oh please," she interrupted, "that's exactly what it was. Eliza Nye is stingy with the servants' rations. According to Arlene, that wasn't the first time she'd heard footsteps, and the cook's always complaining that food's been pilfered. Now I know what you're trying to do, but it won't work. I wasted a whole afternoon today listening to that silly girl complain, and what's worse, I've got to waste part of my morning tomorrow taking the goose a pair of my old gloves."

"Why are you givin' 'er your gloves?" Smythe asked curiously.

"Because she doesn't have any and winter's coming." Betsy stepped away from him. "And you've bought me half a dozen pairs, so I thought I'd give the poor girl a pair of my old ones." She gave him a smile. "Now get off with you. I know you've got to go do some mysterious errand and then go to Howard's for the carriage. Don't worry about me, I'm not going to spend the day fretting."

"You promise?" He was dead serious. He hated it when Betsy was upset.

She gave him a dazzling smile. "I promise."

The night was cold and quiet. Smythe pulled the carriage up in a quiet, deserted spot near the railroad tracks just beyond Dunbarton Street. He tied the reins to a post and patted Bow's nose. "Be quiet now, fella. We'll be back soon. You keep Arrow from frettin' if a train goes rattlin' past."

"You talk to them 'orses like they was people," Wiggins said.

"And they understand every word I say," Smythe retorted. "Come on, it's this way. I found a shortcut over the tracks." He led the way past a set of abandoned build-

ings and over the railway toward Fulham. A few moments
later, they emerged at the bottom end of Dunbarton Street.

"How'd you know about this . . ." Wiggins asked excitedly.

"Shh . . . we've got to be quiet." Smythe hissed.

Hatchet pointed to the end of the row of houses. "I'll
go along and check the back windows."

"We'll do the front." Smythe and Wiggins hurried
along the street to the Geddy house. Wiggins, keeping a
sharp lookout over his shoulder, tried the two front windows. He gave his head a negative shake.

Smythe was fairly sure the back ones would be locked
tight as well. "Keep a sharp eye out, lad." He dropped to
his knees and pulled a flat leather case out of his coat
pocket.

Hatchet, his feet making hardly a sound, joined them
in the front garden. "No luck at the back," he whispered.

"Any lights come on?" Smythe directed his question to
Wiggins, who was acting as the lookout.

"Windows still as black as coal."

Smythe opened the case. A row of gleaming flat metal
devices, some with flat edges and some with long thin
prongs, were nestled against the felt lining inside of the
case.

"Where did you get that?" Hatchet whispered. "No,
don't tell me, I don't want to know."

"Cor blimey, what is that?" Wiggins gasped.

"It's a lockpickin' kit," Smythe said softly. "And I've
got to return it tomorrow." He mentally thanked Blimpey
Groggins for coming through on such short notice. That
had been his most important errand this evening. "Now
let's see if we can get this lock opened. Keep a sharp
lookout, Wiggins, I don't want to get caught with this."

He pulled out an instrument with a long, thin spoke at
one end and inserted it into the lock, just as Blimpey had
instructed him in today's quick lesson on housebreaking.
Turning it softly, he tried to "feel" the tumblers. Nothing
happened. Smythe drew a breath, took the prong out, rein-

serted it and tried again. Blast a Spaniard, it seemed so easy today at Blimpey's. He tried turning the prong in the other direction, felt it hit something and then increased the pressure until he felt the lock click, then click again. "That's it," he murmured. "We're in."

They were back at Upper Edmonton Gardens by a quarter to eleven. The women were sitting at the kitchen table. There was a pot of tea waiting for them.

"We got it." Smythe held up the heavy, cream-colored envelope and handed it to Mrs. Jeffries.

They all took their seats.

"Smythe's got a lockpickin' kit," Wiggins announced. "He's ever so good at it, got that door open in two shakes of a lamb's tail."

"Don't be daft, boy." Smythe glared at Wiggins. "We got lucky, and I told ya, that kit's not mine. I've got to return it tomorrow." He wanted to box the boy's ears. He didn't want Betsy or Mrs. Jeffries to start asking the wrong kind of questions about who'd given him the kit. But then again, both of them would probably approve of Blimpey. He was a scoundrel, but he was a scoundrel with principles.

"I won't ask who you have to return it to," Mrs. Jeffries said with a smile.

"Neither will I," Betsy agreed.

"Is it safe to read the letter?" Hatchet asked. "Has the inspector retired for the night?"

"He came home late and went right up to bed," Mrs. Jeffries replied.

"He didn't even have dinner," Mrs. Goodge added, "and I had Lancashire hot pot."

"Should I open it?" Now that she had it in her possession, she was suddenly uncertain. What they, she, was doing was illegal. What if the letter was something else, something that had nothing to do with the murder?

"Of course you should open it." Luty poked her in the arm. "You read it first, if it don't have nothin' to do with

the killin', we'll put it in a new envelope and whip it right
back into Frieda Geddy's front hall. But iffen it does have
somethin' to do with the killin', then you read it aloud to
the rest of us."

Mrs. Jeffries gave the elderly American a grateful
smile. "There are moments, Luty, when I think you can
read my mind." She picked up the letter opener she'd
brought downstairs, slit open the envelope and pulled out
one folded sheet of paper. Opening it, she began to read.
"It's a confession," she looked up at them. "Shall I read
it aloud?"

"Go ahead," Luty urged. "We're all ears."

*"For the good of my immortal soul, I, Oscar Daggett,
do hereby make this confession of my own free will. I
confess that on September 3rd, 1875, I entered into a
conspiracy with Harrison Nye to defraud Frieda Geddy
out of her rightful share of the gold mine known as
'Transvaal Mine Number 43.' We perpetrated this fraud
by knowingly witholding information as to the value of
the mine from Frieda Geddy after the death of her father,
Viktor Geddy . . ."*

Mrs. Jeffries read the rest of the statement. In it, Daggett detailed how he and Nye had discovered the rich
veins of gold and deliberately kept the information from
Viktor Geddy. But before they could buy Geddy out, he'd
been killed when his wagon had lost a wheel coming
down a steep incline. Daggett hinted that he thought Nye
had something to do with Geddy's accident—he had no
proof, but he was suspicious of Nye nonetheless. With
Viktor Geddy dead and in his grave, it had been an easy
task to buy his share of the mine from his grief-stricken
daughter for the price of a third-class passage back to
England. They'd worked the mine for a couple of years
and made a huge amount of money. But Daggett had always felt guilty about what they'd done. *"In closing, I
can only ask for your forgiveness. I will be held account-
able for my actions soon enough, in that court from which
there is no escape and in front of the One who judges us*

*all. I can only offer the feeblest of excuses for keeping
silent these long years: fear and greed. Pray forgive me
and pray for my immortal soul.*

"*I remain your most repentant servant,*

"*Oscar Elwood Leander Daggett*"

"Cor blimey, if anyone had a reason to kill Harrison
Nye, it would be Frieda Geddy," Wiggins exclaimed.

"But she's been gone for two months, and she never
saw the letter," Betsy pointed out. "So you can count her
out as a suspect."

"I think the only person who could have done it is
Oscar Daggett," Luty said.

"I agree." Mrs. Jeffries looked at the American, her
expression curious. "But I'd be most interested in hearing
your reasons."

Luty smiled wanly. "I'm old and a lot closer to death
than any of you . . ."

Everyone began to argue that point at the same time.

"You're not old," Wiggins protested.

"You're in your prime," Betsy added.

"You're mature," Mrs. Goodge said.

"Madam, really, you're hardly what I would call old,"
Hatchet yelped.

Luty laughed and held up her hand for silence. "You're
all bein' nice, but facts is facts. I'm old. I don't dwell on
it, but I've made my peace with the grim reaper. That's
why I think that Daggett must be the killer. He was trying
to make his own peace."

"I don't think I understand," Betsy said.

"For fifteen years Daggett felt guilty for what they'd
done to Frieda Geddy but he didn't do anything about it
because of fear and greed. I can understand the greed,
after all the fella's a crook. But Daggett also said he was
afraid."

"I should think that was quite understandable as well,"
Hatchet said calmly. "He did a terrible thing."

"Course he did." Luty bobbed her head in emphasis.
"But so what? What did he really have to be afraid of?

Even if Frieda Geddy found out they'd defrauded her from her share of the mine, she couldn't prove it. Not after fifteen years and not without Daggett's very own statement."

"I get it," Wiggins cried. "He must not 'ave been worried about bein' a crook because the only way anyone would know he was a crook was if he admitted it himself."

"Right. From what we've learned about Nye, the fellow wasn't stupid. He wouldn't have left any real evidence of the crime lyin' around for Frieda Geddy or anyone else to find."

"So that means he must have been scared of something else?" Mrs. Goodge mused.

"That's what I think," Luty agreed. "Ask yourself. If he felt so danged bad about defraudin' Frieda Geddy, why hadn't he helped the girl out some in all this time? I think it was because he was scared of Nye. I'll lay ya odds that Harrison Nye had ordered him to stay away from Frieda Geddy, and that's exactly what Daggett did for fifteen years. Then he thinks he's dying, so he writes this letter confessing to what they'd done. He finds out he ain't dying, but the girl who he gives the letter to for delivery goes missing so he thinks that Frieda Geddy already has it in her hands. Scared, he hightails it to Nye's place to tell him what he's done."

"But why would he do that if he was so scared of Nye?" Betsy asked.

"Because he knew good and well how Nye would react. He knew he'd go after the letter. I think Daggett lay in wait for him to arrive at Frieda Geddy's house, then he stabbed him in the back. It's a coward's way of killin', and even Daggett admits he's a coward." She crossed her arms over her chest and looked quizzically at the housekeeper. "Well, how'd I do?"

"I couldn't have said it better myself." Mrs. Jeffries laughed. "That's precisely what I thought must have happened."

"So if Daggett killed Nye, and the only evidence we have linking him to the crime is this letter"—Hatchet nodded at the sheet of paper now lying on the table—"how do we get it to the inspector?"

"We don't," Mrs. Jeffries replied. "Smythe has already told us that Frieda Geddy is returning home. I'm sure she'll find out about the murder before she's been home an hour."

"And once she hears about Nye's murder, she'll put two and two together and give the letter to the inspector herself," Wiggins said triumphantly.

"Aren't you forgetting something?" Mrs. Goodge pointed out. "How can she be giving the inspector a ruddy thing if we've got the letter?"

"We'll have to put it back," Mrs. Jeffries said. "But I don't think we need do that tonight." She looked at Smythe. "Did you find out when Miss Geddy is coming home?"

"I'm not rightly sure," he admitted. "But I think I can find out tomorrow mornin'."

She thought for a moment. It was imperative that the letter be back in that house before Frieda Geddy returned home. Yet she didn't want to send the men back tonight. She wasn't certain it was a good idea to send them back at all. They'd been lucky once, and no one had seen them gain entry. They might not be so fortunate the next time. But the letter must go back. It was the only way.

"What are we goin' to do about the envelope?" Wiggins asked. "The top's been sliced open."

"We'll get another envelope," the housekeeper replied. "You can run down to Murray's tomorrow."

"I've got stationery just like this stuff at home," Luty cut in, "I'll bring it by tomorrow mornin' early."

"That's an excellent idea," Mrs. Jeffries said. "Then we can get the letter safely back to Fulham tomorrow night."

Mrs. Jeffries was waiting in the dining room the following morning when the inspector came down for breakfast.

"Good morning, sir," she said cheerfully. "I trust you slept well."

He raised his hand to his mouth to hide a wide yawn. "Very well. I am famished, though."

"You had a long day yesterday, sir," she said as she poured him a cup of tea.

He pulled out his chair, sat down and took the silver domed lid off his plate. "Ah, wonderful, eggs and bacon. I can see that Mrs. Goodge has given me extra rashers this morning. Give her my thanks. She has an uncanny way of knowing when I'm going to be especially hungry."

Mrs. Jeffries didn't think there was anything uncanny about the cook's abilities. When the inspector was too tired to eat dinner, it meant that he'd be starving by breakfast. But she could hardly tell him that. "She's an excellent cook, sir. She's always trying to anticipate your every need."

Betsy stuck her head in the dining room. "Constable Barnes is here," she announced.

"I didn't hear the doorbell ring," Witherspoon said as the constable came through the door.

"I came in the kitchen door, sir," Barnes explained. His expression was grave. "I was in a hurry, so I cut through your garden."

"What's wrong, Constable?" Witherspoon half rose from the table.

Barnes waved him back into his seat. "Nothing's really wrong, sir. But I do have some information. Yesterday a hansom driver by the name of Neddy Pifer went to the Hammersmith Police Station and made a statement. He took a man fitting Oscar Daggett's description from the corner of Chapel Street and Grosvenor Place. That's less than half a mile from Nye's house. He dropped him at a small hotel on Hurlingham Road, just around the corner from the Geddy place."

"Did the driver get a good look at the fare?"

"He did, sir. Late at night, the drivers are extra careful. They remember faces. He's sure he can identify him. I've made arrangements to take him along to Daggett's house this morning."

Witherspoon frowned slightly. "Gracious, that is rather important. I suggest we bring a few lads along, Constable."

"Are we going to arrest Daggett?" Barnes asked.

"I'm not sure."

"But we've so much evidence against him, sir," Barnes argued. "He had a motive, sir, and no alibi for the time of the murder. If that driver identifies Daggett, he'll have opportunity as well."

Mrs. Jeffries desperately wanted to ask what motive they thought they had for Daggett being the killer, but she didn't dare.

Betsy had no such inhibitions, though. "Why would he want to kill his friend?" she asked. Then she blushed prettily. "Oh, I'm sorry, I didn't mean to step out of my place, sir. But you know how we all follow your cases so closely."

Witherspoon waved her apology off with his fork. He was now shoveling his breakfast in at an alarming rate. "Not to worry, Betsy," he said around a mouthful of egg. "Naturally, you're all curious . . ."

"His motive was very simple," Barnes interjected. "Nye had called him a fool and threatened to kill Daggett when they were together in the study that night. One of the guests had gone to the water closet which was next to the room they were in; he didn't hear the whole conversation, just the end of it. We figure Daggett thought it was either him or Nye."

"Excuse me, Constable." Mrs. Jeffries now thought it safe to ask a question. "But why did this hansom driver wait so long before coming forward? You generally make it known immediately that you'd like to know if anyone took a fare to the area of the murder."

"He was in hospital," Barnes said. "Food poisoning. He found out from the dispatcher this morning that we were making inquiries about fares to Fulham for that night."

Witherspoon shoved the last bite of bacon in his mouth and stood up. "Let's get going then. Mrs. Jeffries, I may be home quite late tonight."

"I'll wait up for you, sir," she assured him.

As soon as he was gone, she looked at the maid. "Gracious, this is a fortunate turn of events."

Betsy nodded. "It looks that way. Oh drat, I forgot to tell you. Luty's downstairs. She'll want to know the latest development." She began clearing up the table, placing the dirty dishes on the tray she'd brought in earlier.

"We'll have a meeting," Mrs. Jeffries said cheerfully. "If Luty's here, Hatchet is as well. If Smythe and Wiggins are still here, we'll tell everyone an arrest is imminent."

"Do you mind if I don't stay?" Betsy yanked the serviette off the table, wadded it up into a ball and put it on the tray. "I've got to take those gloves over to Arlene at the Nye house."

"I don't mind. I'll tell the others where you've gone."

"Thank you, Mrs. Jeffries, I don't like missing one of our meetings, even when we know an arrest is coming, but I did promise Arlene."

Mrs. Jeffries picked up the heavy tray. "You run along now. If you hurry, you might be back before we finish."

Betsy smiled gratefully. "I'll be back before you know it." She hurried out into the hall, hesitated a split second, then charged up the front steps to her room. She'd left the gloves on her bed.

It took her less than five minutes to gather her coat and hat and be out the door. Betsy was very lucky. The omnibus was just trundling up to the stop when she got to Holland Park Road. Half an hour later, she was ringing the bell on the servants' entrance of the Nye house.

Arlene opened the door. "Oh, you came. I was afraid you wouldn't. Come on in, then." She led Betsy across the narrow hall into the servants' hall. Betsy could hear the muted sounds of people coming from the kitchen.

"I told you I'd be here," Betsy said. "Here, these are for you." She handed Arlene the small, flat parcel she'd wrapped in brown paper the night before. It contained two pairs of gloves.

"Thanks ever so much." Arlene took the parcel and pulled off the string. "Oh, there's two pairs here. This is so nice of you. I don't know what to say."

"Don't say anything," Betsy said. "Just accept them and use them." She looked around the servants' hall. "Is it always so quiet here?"

Arlene made a face. "We're supposed to be a house in mourning. Mrs. Nye's got the butler and the footman up in the attic trying to find the crepe so we can drape the windows with it."

Betsy rolled her eyes. "But no one does that anymore."

"Come on"—Arlene rose to her feet—"I'll show you. She's got the downstairs dining-room windows draped already."

Betsy was curious. She got up. "I don't want to get you in trouble."

"Don't worry, no one will see us." Arlene giggled.

Betsy started for the hall, but Arlene grabbed her arm. "Not that way." She dashed over to the far side of the servants' hall. The wall was paneled halfway up its height in a row of wide oak panels. "See this." She pointed to a small, brass latch on the top of the last panel, pressed it and the panel swung open like a small door.

"It's a door," Betsy exclaimed.

"Most people don't even know it's here," Arlene confided as she ducked inside.

Betsy followed her. They went up a small, narrow set of stairs. "Is this a secret passage?"

"Not really," Arlene whispered over her shoulder. "This used to be a shortcut to the dining room from the kitchen. Made getting the food upstairs while it was hot much easier. It's only one story, it just goes up to the dining room. But they walled it up years ago when the old master stopped receiving."

"Do the Nyes know about it?" Betsy asked. They reached the top of the dark stairwell.

"Mrs. Nye does, I saw her comin' out of it early one mornin'. But I never saw Mr. Nye use it." Arlene reached up, feeling for the brass latch that opened the door. She froze at the sound of voices.

Someone was in the dining room.

"What do you mean she's coming back?" Eliza Nye's voice rang loud and clear. "I thought you said she was in Holland with her relatives."

"She was." The voice that replied was a male's. "But she's coming back tonight."

Arlene began edging backward. "Bother, we've got to get out of here."

Betsy had no choice but to ease backwards down the steps. She strained to hear what was going on behind the wall.

"When did you find that out? You should have told me immediately. We'll have to make plans . . ." Eliza's voice trailed off as footsteps sounded into the dining room.

"Get a move on," Arlene whispered frantically at Betsy. "If she's in the dining room, that means the butler's on his way downstairs. I've got to get back to work or I'll be sacked."

Betsy dearly wanted to hear what was happening on the other side of the wall, but she didn't dare argue with the girl. She edged backwards and down another step.

"Hurry up," Arlene whispered.

"Hold on," she hissed, "it's dark."

But Arlene was in no mood for dallying and before Betsy could hear another word, she was down the shallow staircase and back in the servants' hall. Blast her luck.

CHAPTER 10

―――◆◇◆◇◆―――

"Shouldn't we wait for Betsy?" Smythe asked, glancing hopefully toward the back stairs.

Mrs. Jeffries pulled out her chair and sat down. "She isn't coming. She had an errand to run." Even though the meeting hadn't been formally arranged, everyone else was present.

Smythe frowned but said nothing. Maybe the lass was getting her own back because he'd sneaked off yesterday without telling her where he was off to.

Mrs. Jeffries ducked her head to hide a smile. She knew what it cost the coachman to hold his tongue. He was ridiculously overprotective of Betsy and she, of course, delighted in being as independent as possible. She decided to put him out of his misery. "Betsy's doing a good deed. She's taking a pair of her old gloves to a friend who hasn't any. She ought to be back by lunchtime."

"Oh yeah, she told me she had to do that today." He felt a bit ashamed of himself for thinking that Betsy could be so childish. Of course she'd not try to get back at him. She was too good for that sort of behavior.

"That's right nice of 'er," Wiggins said cheerfully.

"Indeed it is," the cook agreed.

"It's a stroke of luck that Luty and Hatchet dropped by," Mrs. Jeffries said. "We've some news. Constable Barnes came by while the inspector was at breakfast. They're going to arrest Oscar Daggett."

"Arrest him?" Hatchet exclaimed. "On what grounds? They don't have the letter."

"They don't need it," she replied. "They found a hansom driver who remembers taking Daggett to Fulham on the night of the murder." She gave them the rest of the details. "So you see, it probably wasn't as imperative as we thought to get that letter back into Miss Geddy's hallway. Sorry, Wiggins, if we'd known about the arrest, I wouldn't have had to rouse you this morning so early."

"That's all right, Mrs. Jeffries." Wiggins laughed. "Me and Fred 'ad us a nice adventure."

They'd decided to use a ruse to get the letter back into the Geddy house. Early that moring, Wiggins and Fred had made their way to Dunbarton Street and Wiggins had surreptitiously tossed Fred's ball into the front garden, specifically, right at Frieda Geddy's front door. Of course, Fred chased it and that, in turn, gave Wiggins an excuse to go all the way up the walkway of the house in pursuit of his errant dog. Once he was within range of the postbox, it had been easy to slip the letter back inside.

"So I was right." Luty slapped her hand against the table top and laughed. "Nell's bells, I just love bein' right."

"So we see, madam," Hatchet said dryly. "Are we sure that Daggett really is the killer?"

"You can't stand it, can ya?" Luty poked him in the ribs. "You just hate it when I'm right."

Hatchet was unperturbed. "Nonsense, madam. I rejoice in the fact that you've made what is apparently, a lucky guess."

"Lucky guess," Luty yelped. "Guessin' had nothin' to do with it."

"Now, now, Luty," Mrs. Jeffries interrupted. "Hatchet's simply having a bit of fun with you. But in answer to his question, all I can say is that it certainly seems as if Oscar Daggett is the killer. As Luty aptly pointed out last night, he certainly had a reason."

"That's too bad," Wiggins interjected. "Oh, I don't mean it's too bad they know who the killer is, I mean it's too bad they found out so quickly. I 'eard ever so much about Miss Geddy this mornin'. I found out where she'd been mailin' them packages off to."

"What packages?" Mrs. Goodge asked absently.

"The ones she 'ad the dustup with the bloke from the post office about," Wiggins reminded her.

"Oh, yes, of course. Are you goin' to tell us?" Mrs. Goodge asked sharply. She was a tad perturbed as well. Her own contributions didn't amount to much at all. All she'd found out was a bit of silly gossip about the Nye household.

"Rotterdam," Wiggins said proudly. "She's got relatives there. She'll be home tonight, too. Comin' in on the eight-fifteen."

"Cor blimey, boy, who told ya all that?" Smythe asked incredulously.

"Mrs. Moff, her neighbor lady told me." Wiggins laughed again. "She come out when she saw Fred." The dog was lying in a spot of sunshine near the kitchen sink, he raised his head when he heard his name. "Seems Mrs. Moff is right fond of dogs. She and Fred got on nicely, they did. While she was tossin' him his ball, we got to talkin'. She told me ever so much. Too bad it's too late."

"I know what ya mean." Smythe sighed. "When I was over at Howard's this mornin', I found out somethin' interestin' as well."

"What?" Mrs. Jeffries asked. "What did you hear?"

"You know 'ow they rent out gigs and all," Smythe said. "I was givin' Bow a good brush down when I 'eard Bill Cronin, that's the stable master, swearin' a blue streak and poundin' somethin' so 'ard it made the rafters shake.

Bill's a nice bloke, not given to losin' his temper, so I went over and seen what was the matter. He was hammerin' the center of the back wheel of a brougham. Said it'd come in wobbly from a couple of nights back, and that he'd not noticed till a man come around that mornin' wantin' to hire the brougham for tonight. Now Bill's not one for rememberin' things very well. Writes everythin' down on bits of paper and old letters he finds in the rubbish." He paused to take a breath. "He'd laid a piece of paper down on the bale of hay that I was standin' next to and I 'appened to glance at it. I saw the name Lionel Bancroft written on it."

"Lionel Bancroft," Hatchet repeated. "Isn't that Eliza Nye's cousin?"

"Some say he's a bit more than that," Mrs. Goodge muttered darkly.

"That's right." Smythe nodded. "So I asked Bill if Bancroft was the man hirin' the brougham for tonight. He said he was. He told me Bancroft 'ad been a customer for years. He was a bit narked at him, said Bancroft had been the last person to have the brougham out and that he ought to have told him it was wobbly when he brought it back in the last time."

"Too bad we didn't know any of this when we was tryin' to solve the murder," Wiggins said. "It might 'ave come in useful."

"I don't see how," the cook grumbled. "All we learned was that Lionel Bancroft rents broughams and Frieda Geddy sends packages to Rotterdam. None of that has anything to do with Oscar Daggett murdering Harrison Nye. More's the pity. I don't think we solved the murder at all. I think the inspector did it all on his own. Mind you, it's not like we had much to work with."

Mrs. Jeffries understood why the cook was upset. In truth, she was a tad irritated as well. It did seem as if the case had come to an abrupt halt. But she wasn't going to share that sentiment with the others. They had done the best they could, and they ought to be proud of their efforts. "Nonsense, we did as much work on this case as we've ever done in the past, and we ought to congratulate ourselves."

They broke up soon after that, and they all went off to take care of the duties they'd neglected during the investigation.

Wiggins went back upstairs to finish cleaning out the attic, Smythe got out a ladder and tackled the gutters along the back of the house, Mrs. Goodge sorted out the dry larder and Mrs. Jeffries went upstairs to organize the linens.

She had just finished putting the towels in the back cupboard when she heard light footsteps on the back stairs. "I'm sorry it took so long, Mrs. Jeffries," Betsy said as she reached the landing and saw the housekeeper, "but I was in a bit of a silly situation."

"That's quite all right, Betsy." Mrs. Jeffries smiled kindly. She didn't want the girl to feel she had to make excuses about her tardiness. "You're a very reliable person, you don't need to apologize for taking a couple of hours off to visit with your friend."

"But . . ."

She held up her hand as the girl started to protest. "Now you run along downstairs and have a cup of tea and something to eat, you must be famished. And pop your head out the back door and let Smythe know you're back. It'll settle his mind."

"But—"

"Now, run along, Betsy." Mrs. Jeffries ushered her toward the back stairs. "You haven't eaten since breakfast."

Betsy gave up trying to explain. Telling Mrs. Jeffries what she'd overheard at the Nyes' would be silly. What, exactly, had she found out? That some woman was coming home from Holland tonight. What did that prove? The little incident had been exciting, but it hadn't meant anything. Not now that Daggett was going to be arrested.

• • •

There was an air of gloom over the household that afternoon. Mrs. Jeffries went up to her rooms to do the household accounts but didn't get very far along on them. Odd things kept popping into her mind. She couldn't stop thinking about the murder. She closed the ledger and leaned back in her chair.

On the one hand, it did seem likely that Oscar Daggett was the killer, while on the other hand, it didn't. Annoyed with herself, she frowned, but the truth was, Daggett being the killer simply didn't feel right. Yesterday afternoon it had all seemed so right, so logical. Yet somehow, she knew it wasn't. She couldn't think what was wrong with the situation. It wasn't as if they had anyone else in mind as a suspect.

She glanced out the window and saw that evening was drawing close. She pushed back from the small table she used as a desk and got up. She might as well go downstairs and help Mrs. Goodge fix supper. At least a bit of company would keep her from being maudlin.

Mrs. Jeffries was on the first-floor landing when she heard the front door open. "Gracious, sir, we didn't expect you home so early." She continued down the stairs.

"I know I'm too early for supper," he explained as he took off his hat, "but I was rather hoping I could have a substantial tea. I've got to go back to the station tonight and write up the arrest report."

"That'll be very tiring for you." She started toward the back stairs. "If you'll go into the dining room, I'll bring you up a tray."

"That won't be necessary." He fell into step behind her. "I'd just as soon eat in the kitchen. Taking all my meals on my own is so boring."

Mrs. Goodge must have heard them coming, for she was already putting the kettle on the cooker when they came into the kitchen. "Good evening, sir," she said cheerfully. "I'll have something ready for you straightaway."

"Thank you, Mrs. Goodge." He pulled out the chair at

the head of the table and plopped down. "I'm very hungry. We didn't have time for lunch. Oh, do sit down, Mrs. Jeffries, and have a cup of tea with me. As I said earlier, I'm heartily sick of taking all my meals alone."

Mrs. Jeffries shot the cook a quick, helpless look, then pulled out the chair next to him and sat down. "Thank you, sir, that would be very nice." She felt very awkward, letting the elderly cook wait on her.

"And bring a cup for yourself, Mrs. Goodge," Witherspoon called, "we might as well be comfortable."

"Thank you, sir," she replied. "My feet could use a nice sit down, and I'm ever so curious about your murder, sir."

In just a few moments, Mrs. Goodge had a hearty tea of bread, cheese, cold roast beef and currant buns laid out in front of the inspector. "Tuck right in, sir," she said.

The inspector speared a huge hunk of cheese with his fork and then took a bite of bread. Mrs. Jeffries poured their tea and handed the cups around.

The cook waited until Witherspoon had swallowed his food before she asked, "Was Daggett surprised when you arrested him?"

"I don't think so." Witherspoon reached for the butter and slathered some across his bread. "He was waiting for us when we arrived at his home; it was almost as if he knew we were coming."

Mrs. Jeffries felt her heart sink. Daggett must be guilty. "Has he confessed, sir?"

"No and I don't think he's going to, either. He admitted taking a hansom cab to Fulham that night, but he claims he didn't go to the Geddy house at all."

"Then why'd he go to Fulham?" Mrs. Goodge asked.

"He refused to say." Witherspoon sighed. "But he insisted he didn't kill anyone."

Mrs. Jeffries realized that the inspector didn't know about the letter. She was amazed that someone from the Daggett household hadn't mentioned it to the police when Daggett was being arrested. But then again, why would they? But surely Mrs. Benchley would have told the inspector that Nelda Smith had shown up unharmed and married.

"Are you going to question Daggett's servants again?" she asked.

"Probably." He finished off the last of the roast beef. "We need to be absolutely certain no one saw him come home at half past nine on the night of the murder." He sighed. "But I've got to tell you, I have grave doubts about Daggett's guilt."

"Doubts?" Mrs. Goodge repeated. "Why?"

He hesitated for a moment. "I'm not altogether sure. There's nothing I can actually put my finger on, it's just that when he protests his innocence, I can hear the ring of truth in his voice."

"You always think the best of everyone, sir," the cook replied.

"I don't think that's it"—he frowned—"and it's not as if Daggett's a particularly likable sort of fellow. Yet I can't help but think he's telling the truth. I suppose it's because there's something about this case that simply doesn't ring true. Something I'm not seeing or understanding . . ." He shook himself slightly. "I expect that sounds silly, doesn't it?"

"Not at all, sir," Mrs. Jeffries said. She had great respect for the inspector's instincts. "I think your 'inner voice' is trying to tell you something." She racked her brain, trying desperately to think of a way to let him know everything they'd learned about the case in the last two days. But short of just blurting it out, she couldn't think of how to do it.

"Do you really think so?" he asked eagerly. "I was rather thinking along those lines myself. Of course, it's not just my feelings that make me think Daggett might be innocent. As I told you, he readily admitted to taking a hansom to Fulham."

Mrs. Jeffries needed to understand something. "Did he say why Nye went to Fulham that night?"

Witherspoon pursed his lips. "No, and that's one of the

things that I find most baffling about this case. Daggett still won't tell us why he went to visit Nye that night or why Nye went to Fulham. Frankly, until I know the why of it all, it simply doesn't make sense."

The two women exchanged covert glances. Neither of them were certain they ought to say a word about Frieda Geddy and that letter. Not when Freida Geddy would be home in a few hours and able to take the letter to the inspector herself.

"I'm sure you'll sort it out, sir," Mrs. Jeffries finally said. "You always do. Are you going to be formally charging Daggett?"

"I don't really know." He pushed away from the table. "I'm going back to the station to have another go at talking to the man. If he's innocent, then it's imperative he tell me the truth." He stood up and smiled. "Don't wait up for me. I shall be quite late."

Mrs. Jeffries escorted him to the door, then hurried back to the kitchen. She didn't know what to think. Witherspoon thought Daggett was innocent. She was now almost certain that he was correct. Nothing seemed really right about Daggett's arrest. "What time will the others be here?" she asked the cook.

"Luty and Hatchet won't be here at all," Mrs. Goodge replied. "Remember, we decided this morning that as an arrest had already been made there was no need for a meetin' this afternoon. So it'll just be our lot. Why? Do you think the inspector's right and that Daggett is innocent?"

"I think we'd better have another meeting," Mrs. Jeffries said thoughtfully. She glanced at the clock and saw that it was almost half past five. "And the quicker, the better."

"They'll be coming in for supper soon," Mrs. Goodge said as she got down the drippings bowl from the shelf over the cooker, "and we can talk as we eat."

By the time the rest of them came in for supper, Mrs. Jeffries had given the matter of the murder a great deal of thought. She waited until they'd all filled their plates with Mrs. Goodge's fragrant shepherd's pie. "The inspector doesn't think Daggett's guilty," she said, "and neither do I."

"If Daggett didn't do it, who did?" Smythe asked.

"Oh good," Betsy exclaimed, "Now maybe I can tell some of the things I've found out."

Mrs. Jeffries looked at her, her expression incredulous. "You have information you haven't shared?"

"Just a couple of bits and pieces I found out yesterday and this morning," she admitted.

"Why didn't you tell us yesterday, then?" Mrs. Goodge demanded.

"Because it wasn't much of anything, and yesterday everyone seemed to think that Daggett was the killer. Everyone had so much to say that by the time it got around to me, we'd just about run out of steam."

"It's all right, Betsy," Mrs. Jeffries said quickly. "We understand. Now, why don't you tell us what you know."

Betsy felt just a bit foolish for not speaking up when she had the chance. She glanced at Smythe and he gave her a warm, encouraging smile. "It isn't all that much. Arlene Hill, she's the maid that works for the Nyes, she told me that on the night of the murder she heard footsteps on the back staircase."

"And you didn't think that was something we ought to know," Mrs. Goodge said sharply.

"Not really. Arlene's a bit of a talker, if you know what I mean. I spent two hours with her, and she told me quite a bit about the household. Now everything she told me could be true, but I think she tarted things up a bit to make herself sound a little important. She's a very lonely girl; she doesn't have any family to speak of."

"You think she made up a story about hearing them footsteps?" Smythe asked.

Betsy cocked her head to one side, her expression thoughtful. "I think she heard something on the stairs, but I don't think it was footsteps. She probably just heard the house settling. The next morning, when the police arrived and there was a bit of excitement, she convinced herself she'd heard footsteps. I don't think she out and out lies."

"She just adds a bit onto her tales to make 'em more interestin'," Wiggins suggested.

Betsy nodded eagerly. "That's it. That's what I was trying to say. She adds to things more than makes them up. Not that she'd have to make up any tales about what happened this morning when we were stuck in that closed-up stairwell." She gave them the details of her adventure at the Nye house. "So you see, my information wasn't really all that important . . ." Her voice trailed off as she saw the way the others were looking at her. "What's wrong? You're all staring at me like I've got a wart on my nose."

Mrs. Jeffries leaned toward the girl. "Are you sure about what you overheard? Are you certain that Lionel Bancroft told Eliza Nye that the woman was coming home from Holland tonight?"

"Yes, I know what I heard. Why? What's so special about one of their friends coming home from holiday?"

"Maybe it isn't one of their friends they were talkin' about," Smythe said softly. "Maybe it was Frieda Geddy."

"Frieda Geddy?" Betsy exclaimed. "Why would you think that?"

"Because that's where she was mailin' all those packages," Wiggins replied, "and she's got relatives in Holland. Do you think it could be 'er they was talkin' about? If it was, what do you think it means?" he asked the housekeeper.

"I'm not sure." Mrs. Jeffries's mind was working furiously. She took a long, deep breath, willing herself to be calm. She closed her eyes briefly and let her thoughts go where they would. All of a sudden the pieces began to fall into place and another, entirely different picture of the puzzle started to form in her mind.

"Before we get all het up," Mrs. Goodge warned, "keep in mind that Miss Geddy coming home tonight and their friend comin' home tonight could be a coincidence. Lots of people travel these days."

"But Miss Geddy was always sendin' packages to Rotterdam," Wiggins pointed out, "and this woman Betsy overheard 'em talkin' about 'is comin' in from Holland."

"What does that prove?" the cook asked. She reached for the pitcher of beer on the table and poured more into her now-empty glass. "And how would Eliza Nye or Lionel Bancroft know anything about Miss Geddy to begin with? From the gossip we heard, Harrison Nye didn't share his past sins with his wife."

"But it'd be an odd coincidence," Smythe muttered.

"But they do happen," Betsy pointed out.

Mrs. Jeffries remained silent as the argument continued all around her. She was thinking. Everything they'd learned flew in and out of her mind willy-nilly. She didn't try to make sense of it, she simply let the facts come and go as they would.

She looked down at her plate and closed her eyes again, letting the impressions come in their own good time. Oscar Daggett's mad rush to Nye's house after he'd learned he wasn't dying. Harrison Nye's admonitions that his wife wasn't to be disturbed after she'd gone to bed, Lionel Bancroft hiring a brougham, the nightgown hidden in the cupboard by the back door, the gossip about Eliza Nye and Bancroft.

Everything tumbled and swirled about in a seemingly senseless tangle. Facts and ideas pushed and shoved one another for supremacy. Wiggins's question about the origins of the fortune, Frieda Geddy's bitterness, gold from the Transvaal.

"Is there something wrong with the pie?" Mrs. Goodge poked the housekeeper in the arm to get her attention.

Shaken from her reverie, she blinked. "What? What did you say?"

The cook repeated her question.

"I'm sorry." Mrs. Jeffries smiled. "I wasn't paying attention. The pie is excellent." She looked down at her plate.

Mrs. Goodge refrained from asking the housekeeper how she knew as she'd not even had one bite of it. "Well, that's good. We've lemon tarts for afters."

Mrs. Jeffries looked back down at her plate and the room was silent. The others looked at each other, their expressions concerned. They all realized the housekeeper was seriously upset. After a few moments, Smythe cleared his throat, and asked, "Mrs. Jeffries, is somethin' amiss?"

"I'm not sure," she replied. She looked over at the carriage clock on the top of the pine sideboard. "It's just past six," she muttered, "and I'm probably mistaken." But she knew she wasn't. She knew it as surely as she knew her own name.

"Are ya sure?" Wiggins pressed anxiously. "You've not touched a bite of your supper."

She raised her head to find all of them staring at her. "I can't eat," she began, "because I'm worried."

"Worried?" the cook repeated. "What's there to be worried about? Everything's fine. I know we didn't contribute all that much to catching Nye's killer, but sometimes the inspector does get one on his own."

"But that's just it." the housekeeper said urgently. "Even he isn't sure he's caught the right killer."

"Even if Daggett's innocent, there's no need to be concerned. They'll not be hanging the man tomorrow. There's plenty of time to find the real killer," Betsy said.

"But that's just it," Mrs. Jeffries glanced at the clock again. "If I'm right, there isn't. If we don't move quickly, there's going to be another murder tonight."

Wiggins put down his fork and pushed back from the table. "Then we'd best get moving. What do you want me to do?"

Smythe was getting to his feet as well. "Just tell us, Mrs. J, and we'll get right on it."

She was touched by their faith in her. "Before we do anything, I have to admit that I'm not one hundred percent certain I'm right, and if I'm wrong now, it could be very embarrassing for the inspector." And for us, she thought, but she knew they already understood that.

"It's a risk I'm willing to take. You've been right often enough in the past," the coachman said easily. "Now you just give us our instructions and we'll get moving. We must be in a 'urry or you wouldn't keep lookin' at the clock."

Mrs. Jeffries made up her mind. She wouldn't risk a human life because she didn't have the courage to act. If she was wrong, she'd pay whatever price needed to be paid. The others obviously had faith in her. "We are in a hurry. We've got to get the inspector to Frieda Geddy's house by the time she gets home tonight."

"She's not arrivin' before eight-fifteen," Wiggins reported eagerly. "So we've got time."

"Is her train arriving at the station or is that the time she's arriving home?" Mrs. Jeffries pushed her plate away and stood up.

Wiggins hesitated for a split second, "Cor blimey, I don't know for certain, but I thought it was the station."

She turned her attention to Smythe. "Do you know what time Bancroft is picking up the brougham?"

"Not really, but I can nip over to Howard's and find out."

She thought for a moment. "That's a good idea. If he's already picked up the carriage, get over to Dunbarton Street and keep an eye on things. If Bancroft gets to Frieda Geddy before the inspector arrives, he'll try and kill her. So keep a sharp eye out for his brougham. Try and stay out of sight if you can." She looked at Wiggins. "Get over to Knightsbridge and tell Luty and Hatchet what's happened. Tell Luty to come along here and tell Hatchet to get to Dunbarton Street."

"Should I go with 'im?" Wiggins asked eagerly. He reached down and patted Fred on the head. The dog sensed the air of excitement that had begun to build in the kitchen and fairly danced at the lad's heels.

"By all means, but make sure you stay out of sight as well. If our plan works, the inspector should be along shortly after Miss Geddy arrives home. But for this to work, timing is everything, so let's keep our fingers crossed." She looked at the cook. "If Wiggins is successful, Luty ought to be along soon. Tell her what's going on—"

"And exactly what's that?" Mrs. Goodge asked, her expression puzzled.

"Oh dear, haven't I said? I am sorry. I think that Lionel Bancroft and Eliza Nye are going to attempt to kill Frieda Geddy tonight. Probably as soon as she gets home. They know about Daggett's letter, you see, and they can't risk that information becoming public."

"What are you going to tell the inspector?" Smythe asked the housekeeper. "I mean, when he trots along to Frieda Geddy's house and Bancroft's not there yet, what's goin' to happen?"

Mrs. Jeffries bit her lip. She hadn't thought about that yet. She'd put the plan together on the assumption that Bancroft would show while the inspector was in the Geddy house. "I'm not sure. I think, perhaps, our best hope is Constable Barnes. If he's with the inspector, I've a feeling he'll keep him hanging about the Geddy house until something happens. You'd best hurry, Smythe. We're running out of time."

Smythe nodded and took off toward the back door.

She turned to Betsy. "Come along, let's get our coats and hats. We're going to the station." She hoped her assessment of Barnes was right. She was fairly certain he knew that she and the others helped on the inspector's cases. If he knew that Mrs. Jeffries had been the one to come to the station with an urgent message, he'd make sure the inspector stayed on Dunbarton Street long enough to make an arrest.

"The station!" Betsy leapt to her feet delighted she was going to be part of the adventure and not just sitting around the kitchen waiting for the men to come home. "We're going to see the inspector?"

"Indeed we are and you'd best put on your thinking cap. By the time we get there, we're going to have to come up with a good story to get him to Dunbarton Street in time."

CHAPTER 11

Witherspoon was dreadfully tired, but he knew his duty. "I suppose I'd best go along to Dunbarton Street and see what the problem might be," he said to Barnes as they came out of the station. "It's late, though, and I think your good wife must be waiting for you. There's no reason for both of us to go. I can handle whatever it is Miss Geddy needs."

"Mrs. Jeffries said the street arab claimed it was a matter of life and death. She said the boy had gotten his instructions from someone in the Nye household, sir. I don't like the sound of that." Barnes wasn't going to let the inspector go to Fulham without him. "My wife's used to my odd hours, sir."

"That's very commendable, Constable." Witherspoon peered up the darkened street, hoping to see a hansom. "But do keep in mind that people often exaggerate, and the boy could even have got the message wrong."

"True, sir. But if Mrs. Jeffries came all the way here to tell us, I think we'd best assume it's serious. Your housekeeper's a very sensible woman. She's not easily fooled. As a matter of fact, sir, I took the liberty of asking a couple of the lads to meet us at Dunbarton Street."

The constable was not as innocent as his inspector. He knew perfectly well that when Witherspoon's household began relaying mysterious messages from street arabs about "a matter of life and death," that they'd best be on their toes. Whether the inspector realized it or not, they were probably going to catch the real killer tonight.

"There's a hansom, sir." Barnes put his fingers to his mouth and whistled.

Startled by the sudden sound, Witherspoon jumped. "Uh, well, if you think it's necessary, then I suppose it'll not do any harm."

The hansom pulled up to the curb, and they climbed on board. "Fulham, please," Witherspoon called to the driver. "Number thirteen Dunbarton Street." He sighed and settled back against the upholstery. "I really don't know why people persist in coming to my house," he murmured. "It seems that on every case I've had lately, someone's popped up at my front door with a message or a telegram or a note. You'd think they'd come to the station, wouldn't you? Seems to me that would be far more efficient."

"As Mrs. Jeffries said, sir, there are a number of people in our city who don't like the police or police stations."

"But it's our job to protect our citizens. I just don't understand why so many of them seem to view us as the enemy."

"They don't view you as the enemy," Barnes said. "As Miss Betsy pointed out, you've built a reputation amongst the, how did she put it, the less-than-fortunate, for being fair and honest."

Witherspoon shrugged modestly. "But most police officers are fair and honest. I've done nothing special." Nonetheless, he was pleased.

Barnes turned his head and rolled his eyes heavenward. Inspector Witherspoon amazed him. After all this time, the man was still as naive as a babe in arms. "Believe me, sir, there's plenty of coppers out there that would give the less-than-fortunate short shrift. But I can see your concern, sir. I expect it's not very pleasant for your staff to have strangers bangin' on your front door all the time. But you've got to admit a lot of our cases have been solved with the help of these people. You know what I mean, sir, people who don't want to be seen helpin' the police, so they do it anonymously by sending along a message to your house." Of course, he knew good and well why all these "people" came to the inspector's house. But he wouldn't share that information with his superior. That would take all the fun out of it. If the truth were known, his own career had done nicely since the inspector had become so adept at solving murders. As the inspector's right-hand man, he'd become a bit of a legend himself.

"They don't mind." Witherspoon waved his hand dismissively. "My household is very interested in my work. I'm very lucky in that regard. They do tend to be a bit overly protective of me though. You know, you're not the only one who thinks Inspector Nivens isn't to be trusted. Mrs. Jeffries has never liked the fellow. Why, by the way, I haven't seen him about much lately. Where's he got to?"

Barnes grinned. "He's kept himself scarce ever since you complained to the chief inspector that he was interferin' on your case."

Witherspoon winced. "I did hate doing that. But I do believe you were right, Constable. Inspector Nivens does seem to resent me very much these days."

"Not to worry, sir. Rumor has it he'll be going up to Yorkshire soon," Barnes replied. "They needed some help on a string of housebreakings that the local fellows can't solve." He didn't tell the inspector that the gossip in the ranks was that Chief Inspector Barrows had gotten fed up with Nivens's playing politics all the time, so he'd sent the fellow off to get him out of Barrows's hair for a few days. "And I must admit, sir, I think you're right about Daggett. I don't think he did it either."

"You and I are the only ones that think he's innocent. I expect it's because he's not a very likable sort." He sighed. "If we want to catch the real killer, we'll have to keep on digging."

"Oh, I don't expect we'll have to dig very far," Barnes murmured softly.

"Cor blimey, I can't see a ruddy thing," Wiggins complained. "We're too far away."

They were flattened against the far side building at the end of the row of homes on Dunbarton Street. They weren't positioned to see Frieda Geddy's home very easily as it was halfway up the block.

"There aren't many hiding places about," Smythe muttered. "And we don't dare be seen. Lower yer 'ead, Wiggins, you're blockin' my view."

"What will we do if things begin to happen, and the inspector's not here?" Hatchet asked softly.

"We'll do what's needed," he said. He turned and gazed at Hatchet's coat pocket. The butler, fully understanding, nodded in the affirmative and patted the pocket. Inside was a small, but deadly derringer. "I brought it. You?"

Smythe looked at Wiggins, who wasn't paying any attention to their conversation, and then back at Hatchet. "I've something with me." He cut a fast glance down to his right boot. Like Hatchet, he'd come prepared. He'd brought his old hunting knife from his days in the Australian outback. It was strapped snugly against his right shin. He hoped for all their sakes he didn't have to use it.

"Cor blimey," Wiggins hissed excitedly, "there's a hansom coming."

Smythe and Hatchet both craned their necks around the corner to get a better view. The hansom pulled up to the front of number 13 and a cloaked figure got down.

"It's got to be Frieda Geddy," Smythe whispered. He was fairly sure the killer was going to arrive by brougham, not by hansom. "Look, she's getting out a carpetbag."

They watched her pay the driver and then head toward the front door. She stood on the doorstep for a moment, and then her front door opened and she stepped inside. A few moments later, a light appeared in the front-room window.

"Look, here comes another hansom." Wiggins pointed down the road as a cab pulled around the corner.

Smythe and Hatchet looked at one another in dismay.

"He's got here early," Wiggins groaned. "What are we goin' to do?"

"We'll 'ang on a bit and see what 'appens," Smythe muttered. He looked at Hatchet and saw his own fears mirrored on the butler's face. "Are you thinkin' what I'm thinkin'?"

"I think that's a safe assumption." Hatchet pursed his lips. "It appears as if our killer isn't going to show himself. Apparently, we've been wrong about this."

"We're not wrong," Wiggins insisted. He'd finally started paying attention. "Mrs. Jeffries is dead on about this. It's the only thing that makes sense. Maybe he just ain't got 'ere yet."

"And that's even worse," Smythe insisted. "Because if the inspector leaves after talkin' to Miss Geddy, the killer'll be able to take his sweet time doin' 'er in and Inspector Witherspoon'll never forgive 'imself."

"Then we'll just have to spend the night here," Hatchet said staunchly, "and make certain that doesn't happen. What's happening now?" he hissed at Wiggins, who'd craned his neck back around the side of the house.

"The hansom's pullin' up to the front of the 'ouse," Wiggins replied. "Ow, that smarts."

"Sorry," Smythe replied. Fearing they'd be seen, he'd pushed Wiggins down a bit harder than he'd intended. "Blast a Spaniard, the inspector and Constable Barnes is gettin' out of the hansom."

"This isn't good," Hatchet said. "I think we're going to be here for the rest of the night."

All of a sudden, the quiet night was filled with a bloodcurdling scream. It came from inside the Geddy house.

Witherspoon and Barnes jumped and raced toward Miss Geddy's front door.

Another scream came again, followed by a harsh cry.

The two policemen reached the front door. Barnes grabbed the knob and twisted. "It's locked, sir."

"Help, help," a woman cried from inside the house. There was a loud crash, and then the sound of breaking glass.

"Break it open," Witherspoon shouted. He and Barnes both took a step back and then shoved their shoulders hard against the door.

About that time, two police constables, hearing the commotion, came racing around the corner.

"Should we do somethin'?" Wiggins asked worriedly. That scream had just about made him faint, but he'd gotten ahold of himself. "It sounds like someone's bein' murdered in there."

"Let's wait a moment," Hatchet replied. He'd caught sight of the two policemen running toward the Geddy house. "I believe there will be plenty of help."

The two constables raced up to the house just as Barnes and Witherspoon took a step back to try again. One of the constables, a big, burly fellow, said, "Let me try kickin' it, sir." He raised his leg and gave a hard kick against the lock just as another scream came from the house. The door flew open and the police rushed inside.

Wiggins, Hatchet and Smythe came out from their hiding place, hoping to hide in the excitement of the moment and the darkness of the night. "Cor blimey, I wish I knew what was goin' on in 'at house . . . cor blimey, who's that?" Wiggins pointed to a figure who'd just come around the corner. But whoever it was hadn't walked around the corner, they'd crept quietly and kept close to the shadows, as though they didn't want to be seen.

Even at this distance, they could see the figure wore a skirt.

She wasn't watching them; she had her attention fixed

firmly on the house midway down the row. Holding her arms stiffly down at her side, she started down the cobblestone street toward the house.

"Who is it?" Wiggins persisted. "And why's she creepin' about like she don't want to be seen?"

"Because she doesn't," Hatchet whispered. "Look, she's heading for the Geddy house." He had a strong feeling they'd better get closer. There was something about the stiff way the woman walked, something about her fixed attention on the house that sent alarm bells ringing in his head.

"What?" Smythe hissed. "You want us to get closer? But what if someone sees us?"

"We've got to risk it," Hatchet persisted. He didn't claim to be psychic or to believe in any of that sort of nonsense, but he knew if they didn't get moving, something awful was going to happen.

Smythe caught something of Hatchet's urgency. "All right, then, let's go." They moved farther out into the street and started walking toward the house. "But you're the one that has to come up with some kind of story when we're caught . . ." He broke off as he saw the woman reach the Geddy house. He also saw why she held her arms so stiffly at her side. She was carrying a revolver in her right hand.

"Blast a Spaniard . . ."

"I know," Hatchet gulped. "I saw it too. Wiggins, go for help. Run and get more police constables; I think we're going to need them."

Inside the house, Witherspoon had plunged ahead of the others. To his right, a curved archway opened into a small sitting room.

"Don't come any closer or I'll slit her throat."

Witherspoon skidded to a halt. The others did as well.

Lionel Bancroft was holding a terrified, middle-aged woman up on her knees by her hair. He held a long, wicked-looking knife at her throat. "I mean it," he snarled. His handsome face was contorted in rage and fear, his hair was askew and a trickle of blood dribbled down his nose.

The room was in a shambles. A chair was knocked over, cushions had been tossed off the settee, and the front of a china hutch had been smashed. The inspector realized that Frieda Geddy had put up a fight. Good for her.

"Let Miss Geddy go," he said calmly. "You don't want to be in any more trouble than you already are."

"Let me go, you great oaf," Frieda Geddy snapped.

"Shut up, you stupid bitch," Bancroft snarled. "It wasn't supposed to happen like this. It was supposed to be easy."

"Now, now, let's not be silly . . ." Witherspoon was terrified the knife was going to slip and sever the woman's neck.

"I said, let me go." Miss Geddy jerked her head to one side and Bancroft lost his grip on her hair. She jammed her elbow back and up as hard as she could. Bancroft screamed in pain, and the knife went flying to one side. Immediately, he was tackled by four policemen.

"Get off of me," Miss Geddy called as she tried to crawl out from the flailing arms and legs of London's finest.

"I've got him," Barnes yelled out. He grabbed Bancroft's collar and heaved the both of them to one side. The two other policemen scrambled to their feet and dived toward Bancroft, grabbing his arms and pinning them behind him.

Witherspoon disengaged his foot from under Freida Geddy's arm. "Are you all right?"

"I'm unharmed," she replied. They were both gasping for air as they staggered to their feet. "Thank God you were here. He tried to kill me . . ." She pointed at Bancroft.

"Take a moment and catch your breath," Witherspoon said. "You've had a dreadful shock."

"He was waiting inside my house," she gasped.

"Are you sure you're unharmed?" Witherspoon per-

sisted as he ran his gaze up and down her person, searching for blood. Barnes, afraid his inspector might be hurt,
had dashed over and was carefully, but surreptitiously doing the same to Witherspoon.

"I'm certain," she replied. She glared at Bancroft, who
was standing between the constables, his expression de-
fiant. "Why was he trying to kill me? Who is he?"

"He's a fool." The words came from the archway and
were spoken by a woman.

Witherspoon and Barnes both whirled about. Eliza Nye
stood facing them. She had a revolver in her hand. It was
pointed at the inspector's head. "Lionel is a weak fool,
but I'm not. I assure you, Inspector, I'll blow your brains
out if you don't let us leave. I'm quite a good shot. I
shan't miss."

Witherspoon swallowed heavily. There was a hard,
crazed look in her eyes. A look that convinced him she
was quite capable of doing precisely as she said. "You're
already in enough trouble, Mrs. Nye. I suggest you put
that weapon down and come along peacefully."

"Trouble?" she laughed. "Don't be a fool, Inspector.
I'm going to hang. I stabbed my husband to death. Now
do as I say, and no one will get hurt."

"You stabbed him?" the inspector exclaimed in surprise. He cast a quick glance at Bancroft. He wasn't quite
sure precisely what was going on here, but he'd sort that
out later. The important thing was to get everyone out of
the house alive.

"Lionel was hardly up to the task," she sneered. "For
God's sake, he can't even do in one lone middle-aged
woman." She waved the gun at Miss Geddy. "But enough
of this. Now listen carefully, Inspector. Order your men
to release Lionel and do it now."

Witherspoon turned and nodded at the constables holding Bancroft. "Step away, lads. We don't want anyone
getting hurt."

As soon as he was free, Bancroft raced across the room.
"I was going to do it," he told her, "but the stupid bitch

put up a struggle. What are we going to do now?" He and Eliza Nye stood with their backs to the door.

"We're going to kill them all and make a run for it," Eliza said bluntly. She took a step forward and aimed the gun at Frieda Geddy. "And she's going to get it first."

"You're a very rude and awful person," Frieda Geddy snapped, "and I certainly hope you'll rot in hell."

Witherspoon, holding out his arms, stepped in front of her. "I'm afraid I can't allow that to happen. Now, please, put the gun down before you hurt someone."

"Good God, you're an even bigger fool than Lionel," Eliza yelped. She leveled the gun at Witherspoon. "All right, then. As you're in such a hurry to die, let's have at it."

Suddenly, Bancroft screamed as he was brought to his knees by a flying tackle. Eliza Nye gasped and whirled around, leaping backwards a bit as the two grappling men crashed into her. Her arms flailed as she struggled to keep her balance. When she righted herself, she was staring down the short, blunt barrel of a derringer.

"Drop your gun, ma'am," Hatchet ordered her. "I assure you, I'm an excellent shot and even if I weren't, at this range, I couldn't miss."

Smythe drug Bancroft to his feet as the room went quiet and everyone's attention turned to the two people with guns. Hatchet's derringer was aimed at Eliza Nye's head, her revolver was down at her side. She hadn't a hope of aiming it before he fired. But still, she didn't drop it.

Eliza Nye and Hatchet stared into one another's eyes. The seconds ticked past and neither of them moved.

"You wouldn't shoot a lady," she said softly. "You're a gentleman."

"I assure you, madam," he replied coldly, "I would. Now drop your weapon."

She smiled slightly and dropped the gun onto the carpet. "I was wrong. You're not a gentleman."

"And you're certainly no lady," he said.

• • •

"Cor blimey, I almost fainted when I saw Hatchet take out that gun." Wiggins could talk about it now that they were safely back at Upper Edmonton Gardens. It was very late, closer to morning than midnight. Everyone, except for the inspector, who'd stayed at the station to finish his report, was gathered around the kitchen table.

"We didn't know what else to do," Hatchet said honestly. "We saw her go into the house, and she was holding that gun like she meant to use it. Smythe and I looked at one another and realized that we had to take action. None of the policemen in that house were armed. They couldn't defend themselves."

"It's a good thing we went in when we did," Smythe said. "She 'ad that bloomin' gun aimed right at the inspector's 'eart. All I could think to do was tackle Bancroft and hope that rattled Eliza Nye enough so she'd make a mistake."

"And she did." Hatchet closed his eyes briefly. "She lowered her gun enough for me to shove my derringer in her face."

"You got the drop on her," Luty clarified. Much as she'd have liked to give her butler a good tongue-lashing on his taking such stupid risks, she couldn't. If she'd been there, she'd have done the same. And truth to tell, she was downright proud of him.

"Do you think the inspector and Constable Barnes believed your story?" Betsy asked. She patted Smythe's arm absently as she spoke. She was so proud of him she could burst, but that didn't mean she didn't want to box his ears for putting himself in harm's way. But they'd talk about that privately.

"I don't know," Smythe replied. "By the time we got to the station, he was so busy takin' statements and chargin' 'em, I'm not sure what he thought."

"I think he was quite relieved when we arrived," Hatchet said. "Our explanation certainly sounded plausible. We went there simply to make sure that Miss Geddy wasn't in danger. After all, we knew the inspector and

Barnes were on their way, Mrs. Jeffries and Betsy had gone to the station with a life-or-death message." He shrugged. "It certainly sounded reasonable to me."

"Yes and wasn't it a happy coincidence that you just happened to have your derringer because Luty insisted you carry it with you when you went out at night," Mrs. Jeffries added with a smile.

Luty snorted. "That's right, blame me. Come on now, Hepzibah, don't keep us in suspense anymore. How'd you figure out it was them two?"

"And how'd you know they was going to try and kill Frieda Geddy tonight?" Wiggins added.

"That part was easy," she replied. "I knew they had to move tonight. They couldn't afford for Miss Geddy to make the contents of that letter public. Not when they'd gone to all that trouble to kill Harrison Nye. When Betsy told us what she'd overheard, I realized they must have been keeping an eye on Frieda Geddy. Probably since Lionel Bancroft eavesdropped on Daggett and Nye the night of the murder."

"How'd you know it was her they was talkin' about?" Luty asked. "Betsy only heard that someone was comin' back from Holland."

"And you'd told us that Frieda Geddy spoke Dutch, and we knew that she was coming home tonight," Mrs. Jeffries explained. "I knew it couldn't be a coincidence. Once they knew that Oscar Daggett had confessed to what he and Nye had done to Miss Geddy fifteen years ago, they made it their business to find out where the woman was and when she'd be coming home."

"Because of the letter?" Hatchet asked.

"Right."

"Why didn't they do what we did and just break into her place and steal it?" Wiggins reached for another bun.

"They were afraid to go back to Dunbarton Street," Mrs. Jeffries replied. "They were afraid someone would see them. I think their plan was to give it a few weeks, to wait until the excitement about the murder had died down, and then steal the letter. But their plan was foiled when Miss Geddy decided to return home."

"I still don't understand how you knew it was them two," Mrs. Goodge said.

"I didn't until tonight." Mrs. Jeffries closed her eyes briefly, thinking of how close she'd come to getting the whole thing wrong. "It was only when Betsy told us about the footsteps on the back stairs and what she'd overheard at the Nye household that I put it all together. You see, they've planned it for ages."

"Who planned what?" Luty demanded. She didn't want to complain, but honestly, sometimes following what Hepzibah was saying was harder than chasing a pig through a corn patch.

"Eliza Nye and Lionel Bancroft. They've planned on murdering her husband for ages. I think they were actually going to do it the night he was killed—that's why Eliza Nye added the names of the Windemere brothers to the guest list. She wanted to make sure there were plenty of suspects for the police to worry about."

"You think she was going to kill him that night anyway?" Betsy asked incredulously. "Now that is a coincidence."

"Maybe not that night, but I think they were planning on doing it soon. That's why she wanted the Windemere brothers back in Nye's life. They were excellent suspects. When Wiggins told us that it was Eliza Nye, not her husband, who put those names on the list, I didn't understand what it meant. But today I realized she'd done it so the police would be looking at them instead of her. The fact that Oscar Daggett came along with his wild story about his confession only helped their plan along."

"But they didn't know about the confession . . ." Betsy frowned. "Did they? I mean, no one knew but Nye and Daggett."

"Yes they did," the housekeeper interrupted. "Lionel Bancroft got up from the dinner table, supposedly to go to the water closet. I expect he did no such thing; I expect he eavesdropped on Nye and Daggett. Also, remember, he'd hired a brougham for that night as well. I think he waited until Nye left, tipped off Mrs. Nye about the change in plans, then the two of them took off for Dunbarton Street."

"I wonder how she got out of the house?" Mrs. Goodge muttered. "The servants all saw her retire."

"And they were, no doubt, too busy cleaning up the dining room to notice that she'd slipped down the back stairs and out the back door. Remember, none of them dared disturb her once her door was closed for the night. That was quite a clever ruse on her part. I expect she'd done it a number of times. As a matter of fact, I imagine that every time Nye went out late at night, Mrs. Nye was hot on his heels and out the door herself."

"How do ya figure that?" Luty asked.

"I'm not certain, of course," Mrs. Jeffries admitted. "But when I found out about that enclosed staircase it all made sense. She needed time to plot and scheme with her cousin, but she could hardly do that in the house because the servants were around all the time. So what does she do? She gives him some nonsensical story about being a light sleeper and insists that no one disturb her after she's retired. Then she slips out whenever she wants by going through the dining room, down that staircase and right out the side servants' entrance. When I heard about the maid getting sacked over the nightdress, it made sense."

"Huh?" Wiggins frowned and scratched his nose.

"Mrs. Nye nipped out whenever her husband did to see her cousin. She kept a nightdress in a cupboard by the servants' back door, at least she did until one of the maids found it—what better than to toss a nightgown over your clothes and pretend to be sleepwalking. That way, if you were seen coming and going, you had an excuse at the ready so to speak."

"But he was her cousin. Why couldn't they see each other openly?" Betsy asked.

"Because they was always plottin' and tryin' to figure

out the best way to kill 'im," Wiggins put in. "Like Mrs. Jeffries said, they daren't do that at 'ome. Someone might overhear 'em."

"But they've been married two years . . ." Smythe muttered.

"I don't think they've met all that many times," Mrs. Jeffries persisted. "But I think they definitely met up on the night of the murder, drove to Fulham in the brougham that Lionel had hired and stabbed him to death before he reached the Geddy house."

"She stabbed him," Hatchet muttered. "She said she didn't trust Lionel to do it right."

"But why?" Betsy persisted. "She didn't have it any worse than lots of other women. Why kill him?"

"Because I think she liked being in control. As long as she was married to Nye, she wasn't. Remember what you told us, Betsy, Nye let her spend his money, but he made her account for each and every penny," Mrs. Jeffries said.

"But why kill Frieda Geddy?" Mrs. Goodge persisted. "With her husband gone, what did it matter that he'd been a thief. She stood to inherit his money, she could have run off with Lionel whenever she liked."

"Maybe not," Mrs. Jeffries replied. "I'm not sure what the law is, but I believe if you build a fortune using money that was obtained fraudulently, which is what Nye did, then the fortune can be divvied up and parceled out to the victims of that fraud."

"In other words, with Oscar Daggett's confession, Frieda Geddy could tie up Nye's estate in court for years," Hatchet said with a satisfied smile.

"Well, we've solved another one." Wiggins leaned back in his chair and yawned. "I think we were right sharp about it too."

"Now we've just got to hope the inspector isn't too annoyed about what all has transpired tonight," Mrs. Jeffries murmured. She cocked her head to one side. "I believe I hear a hansom pulling up now."

They fell silent as they heard his footsteps crossing the

hall and come down the stairs. "Yoo hoo," he called. "Is anyone up . . . oh good, you've waited up."

Mrs. Jeffries relaxed a bit. He didn't seem terribly upset. "Yes, sir. Of course we were keen to know what transpired at the station."

He yawned and took a seat next to Mrs. Jeffries. "Well, it was all a bit muddled at first, neither Bancroft nor Mrs. Nye would make a statement. Finally, Bancroft admitted that they'd conspired to kill her husband. It seems the two of them have been . . . ah . . . close for many years. He's completely in her power. Besotted with the woman."

"So he's confessed." Mrs. Goodge asked.

"Yes. But she hasn't. She hasn't said one word. I don't think she's going to either. She's quite a strong-willed woman. I don't believe she's quite sane." He sighed deeply, then looked around the table. "I want you all to know how deeply grateful I am. If you hadn't been concerned about the welfare of a woman you'd never even met and trotted along to Dunbarton Street to keep an eye on her, a number of us would all be dead."

"We were only doing what was right." Smythe blushed a deep red and looked down at the table.

"We were doing our duty," Hatchet added.

"Cor blimey, I was scared to death," Wiggins admitted.

Witherspoon held up his hand for silence. "All of you did far more than your duty and as for being scared"— he smiled at the lad—"so was I. But I do want to make something absolutely clear. I don't want any of you to ever put yourself in harm's way for me again. If something happened to any of you, I'd never forgive myself."

No one said a word. Finally, the inspector rose to his feet. "But then again, I sincerely hope never to be staring down the barrel of a gun again. Again, thank you all. I don't know what I've done to deserve such loyalty and friendship from all of you, but I want you to know, I thank God for you every single day of my life. Without you, I'd be a lonely middle-aged man living a life of terrible solitude."

Smythe had turned even redder, Betsy was dabbing at her eyes, Mrs. Goodge was choking back tears, Hatchet was holding himself so rigidly he looked like he was going to burst and Luty was staring at the tip of her shoe. Only Wiggins was looking at the inspector, and he was grinning from ear to ear.

Mrs. Jeffries rose to her feet and faced her employer. "Without you, sir, we'd be doing the same."